The

EXPLORER

& OTHER STORIES

Jyrki Vainonen

The Explorer and Other Stories

by Jyrki Vainonen

Cheeky Frawg Books
Tallahassee, Florida

"The Explorer" and The "Pearl" were first published in *Tutkimusmatkailija ja muita tarinoita* (The Explorer and Other Stories) in 1999.

"Blueberries" and "The Fridge" were first published in *Luutarha* (The Boneyard) in 2001.

"The Garden," "The Aquarium," and "The Library" -- were first published in *Lasin läpi* (Through the Glass) in 2007.

ISBN 978-09857904-5-5

Cheeky Frawg is run by Ann & Jeff VanderMeer.
Editorial Assistance: Desirina Boskovich and John Klima

Cheeky Frawg logo copyright © 2011 by Jeremy Zerfoss
Cover and interior design by Jeremy Zerfoss

Cheeky Frawg would like to thank FILI, the Finnish Language Exchange (http://www.finlit.fi/fili/en/), for partially subsidizing the translation of this book.

FILI
FINNISH LITERATURE EXCHANGE

For a complete catalogue of Cheeky Frawg selections, visit:
http://www.cheekyfrawg.com

Cheeky Frawg
POB 4248
Tallahassee, FL 32315
pressinfo@vandermeercreative.com

Contents

Introduction

By Johanna Sinisalo

Ever since I was a little child, I have known that my everyday world is filled with thin, opaque curtains. Though impenetrable, these curtains are as light as gauze, and the slightest breeze, my own breath or even just the right kind of careless thought can sweep them aside. For a fraction of a second, a path opens to some other place, bathed in a strange light. You can step through if you are quick and brave enough. Very often the curtains part just as sleep is creeping upon me in my bed.

When I take that step through the curtains, it first seems like everything around me is the same, but the farther I go, the stranger more disjointed and wondrous that new landscape becomes.

One time after stepping through the curtains, I saw in the distance a strange, hazy figure. He looked human, but had to be one of the indigenous inhabitants of those lands. His name was Jyrki Vainonen.

Jyrki Vainonen lives on the other side, but every once in a while he slips over to visit our world. He parts the curtains as he comes, and if we want, we can peek back over or visit the other side for a while. This book collects these visitations in the form of short stories.

Vainonen's stories start with situations that seem mundane, easily identifiable and very real. I can see, hear, smell and feel familiar details, the settings are recognizable, the characters are doing ordinary things. They are taking care of their neighbor's aquarium, driving a bus, using the bathroom in a library, working at a weather station. Then, almost imperceptibly, a strange, alien and sometimes even frightening presence begins to infiltrate the story.

Jyrki Vainonen—like most of the authors I admire—avoids settling in any one genre or clear tradition. He just opens the way and lets the world he has created seep into the reader. His stories shun definitions— are they fantasy, surrealism or horror? It does not matter. His stories give us flashes of universes ruled by laws all their own. A short visit in each world is like diving into the water and, eventually, coming back to the surface gasping for air.

Vainonen's stories are far from harmless tours where one can just admire the exotic vistas of the worlds behind the curtain. When visiting Vainonen's worlds, one steps deep into humanity and the human soul. Loss that is too great to bear; feelings of foreignness or otherness that define the main character's world; the impotence of intelligence in the face of nature.

One often hears it said that good stories are like icebergs drifting in the sea: there is much more to them than is apparent on the surface. Jyrki Vainonen's stories are just such icebergs, but they drift in a strange sea, one that is foggy, windswept and lit by the skewed light of alien moons.

Johanna Sinisalo is a Finnish writer, who is best known for her novel *Troll: A Love Story*. The novel tied for the James Tiptree Jr. Award in 2004 and has been translated into 15 languages. Of other Sinisalo's novels, *Birdbrain* is available in English, and *The Blood of Angels* will be soon translated. In addition to six novels and two short story collections, she has written a book for children, several screenplays and edited two anthologies, including *The Dedalus Book of Finnish Fantasy*.

The Explorer

Doctor Klaus Nagel, the director of a remote weather station, disappeared on the night of April 6th. The station was located on the outskirts of the city, atop a low crest of rock. The night was windy, low clouds drifted over roofs and tree tops. In the small hours between four and six, it rained. Water dug small furrows into the dirt road that led up to the station. Behind the station, rainwater rolled down the flanks of the rock.

Meteorologist Johannes Dagny, who was working the night shift, was waiting to go home. He sat half-asleep at his desk in the light of a small lamp and stared out into the yard. Every now and then, his head nodded down to his chest, and he woke with a start. In an attempt to stay awake, he got up to stretch his legs and look out the window. Puddles glistened on the uneven yard. Steam rose from the sand. Raindrops sparkled on the branches of the birch tree right outside the window. Dagny was waiting for Dr. Nagel. He longed to see the lights of Dr. Nagel's red Honda appear from behind the hill and for the car to turn into the yard, swaying as it crossed the puddles, sand hissing beneath its tires.

A clock ticked away on the desk. When Dr. Nagel hadn't shown up by seven o'clock, his colleague presumed that he had overslept and decided to wake him.

The phone rang five times, and then he heard a sleepy voice on the other end. It took him a while before he was able to explain to Marianne, Dr. Nagel's young wife, why he was calling, as she had been deep asleep when the ringing phone had woken her up. "Hold on," Marianne sighed into Dagny's ear.

A few moments passed. The morning news was on the radio. Dagny stirred the cold coffee that was congealing in the cup in front of him. Birds were singing in the woods behind the station. He imagined

Marianne shaking her husband awake, handing him the receiver, yawning, stretching her arms, and running her fingers through her dark hair. Dagny had met Marianne once at party hosted by his boss. He would have been happy to exchange places with Nagel and wake up every morning next to a woman like that.

"Hello?" It was Marianne's voice. "He's not here...he must already be on his way."

Dr. Nagel was not on his way to work, however. He was not sitting behind the wheel of his Honda, driving past the market square and the city hall, or turning his car onto the road leading out of the city. After the phone call, Marianne noticed that the clothes that her husband had laid out for work were hanging, carefully folded, over the back of a chair. She slipped out from under her warm blanket and padded barefoot over to the kitchen. Not a soul was there. Not in the hallway or the bathroom, either. After returning to the bedroom and wrapping herself in a robe, Marianne noticed a piece of paper on her husband's nightstand. The note contained a single sentence written in Dr. Nagel's sharp hand: "My dear Marianne! I have vanished from your life to become a part of your life. Klaus."

A few hours later a serious-faced police inspector stood in the Nagels' kitchen, asking Marianne whether she had any idea what the message meant. Marianne shook her head. They heard the sounds of the policemen searching through the apartment: the furniture clattered upstairs as someone moved it, the bookcase was being emptied in the living room. Someone coughed in the bathroom. The young inspector clearly felt uncomfortable. "No need to worry, Mrs. Nagel," he comforted the woman in front of him and lifted his gaze from her chestnut hair to some indeterminate point near the ceiling. "We'll find him."

But the inspector was wrong. Dr. Nagel was not found, even though the investigation was conducted thoroughly and a missing-person bulletin was published in the media. No one seemed to have seen Dr. Nagel after the 5th of April. He had spent that morning at the weather station, and at 3 p.m., the person who had the night shift had relieved him. Nothing unusual had happened during the day before his disappearance. The evening had also passed in a typical fashion, Marianne said. At 11 p.m., Dr. Nagel had kissed her good night and stayed in his study reading a book about the conquest of the North Pole, a book that he'd been engrossed in for the past couple of days. The next morning Mrs. Nagel had woken up alone in their wide marriage bed.

For a moment, the disappearance of Dr. Nagel turned the lives of those it touched upside down. The familiar daily routines at the weather station were thrown into disarray, as work there was constantly interrupted. Reporters, photographers, and news sharks bustled about amid the maps, monitors, and computers. The police hunted for fingerprints with their powder brushes, finding more than enough all over the station. Johannes Dagny had to repeat the events of his shift to the reporters over and over again. He saw himself on television and couldn't help wondering whether that was really how he looked in the eyes of others. The simple act of describing the events momentarily transformed the life of the ever so conscientious Dagny. He came to enjoy the feeling of power he got from sitting in front of the reporters, who hung on his every word. He became more enamored by his own story with each telling and soon began to embellish it with juicy details: the nocturnal rain shower became "the deluge of the century," streams became "rapids," and dull drowsiness into "a slumber populated by strange dreams."

The fuss caused by the disappearance also seemed to bother Marianne. Soon after the disappearance she shut herself in the house and refused to talk to the reporters. The only person she let in was the police inspector. His route did seem to take him rather frequently to Dr. Nagel's house, which stood in a grove of pine trees on the crown of a hill on the outskirts of the city. The inspector's car was seen parked next to the Nagels' red Honda almost daily—even in the evenings, when the blinds had already been drawn and the moon poured its light onto the lawn.

The young wife's reticence was grist for the tabloids' mill. Someone leaked to the press that the Nagels' marriage had been faltering. Marianne was painted as a neglectful, wanton woman, whose hunger for men remained insatiable, even after she'd married Dr. Nagel—

for money, according to the tabloids—a man twenty years her senior, whom she'd then murdered and whose body she'd hidden.

Amidst all the fuss, the investigation was going nowhere. Marianne did, however, notice that her husband's backpack and fishing gear were missing, as were some clothes that he used when he went hiking. The police assumed that Dr. Nagel had, for some reason or another, gone out for a nocturnal hike. The possibility of sleepwalking was also considered, though Marianne claimed that her husband spent his nights sleeping, not walking around. The woods around the city were combed, to no avail. No sign of Dr. Nagel was found.

A couple of weeks after the disappearance, the fuss started to subside. The papers had to come up with new headlines and exposés. In the police archives, the file on the disappearance of Dr. Nagel was moved to a tall metal filing cabinet marked "Unsolved disappearances." No one paid attention any longer to the fact that the inspector's car was now parked in the Nagels' yard every day. No one was interested that Marianne, who still seldom left her home, didn't look grief-stricken, but was glowing like a young bride.

However, there was one person who did get wind of all of this: namely Dr. Nagel. He had disappeared only in that he wasn't found. He wasn't hiding in the woods surrounding his house, using binoculars after darkness had fallen to watch the blinds covering the lit windows as the shadows of his wife and the inspector merged. Neither was he lurking in the basement or garage amid potato sacks, jam jars, toolboxes, and stacks of winter tires, let alone skulking around the house at night, skirting the furniture in the dark to eavesdrop at the bedroom door.

Dr. Nagel had done what he had said he would: he had vanished from his wife's life to become a part of her life. Had the message he'd left been interpreted correctly, he would have been found. On the night of April the 6th, Dr. Klaus Nagel moved in to his wife Marianne's right thigh.

Dr. Nagel chose Wednesday the 5th of April as the day of his departure. When Marianne left that evening for her aerobics class, as she did every Wednesday, Dr. Nagel made the preparations for his expedition in peace and quiet. He decided to take with him only the bare necessities. After all, he was headed to a place with a climate much like that at the Equator. He thus filled his backpack with only a few sets of clothing, some canned food, fishing gear, a volume of the *Home Medical Encyclopedia* (which covered the human vascular system), and the equipment he would need for his research—a thermometer, an anemometer, a barometer, and a plastic cylinder for measuring the amount of precipitation.

Dr. Nagel hid the backpack under the bed. Content, he then settled down with a book and waited for his wife to return. He knew that when she returned, the first thing she would say would be "That was one tough class, I'm completely exhausted," and later she would drop another hint "I'm so tired... I'll probably fall asleep as soon as I close my eyes." And so it happened: Marianne fell asleep while her husband was still reading about the adventures of arctic explorers, while he was roaming the snowy wastes with a cloud of vapor from his breath surrounding his head, plucking ice crystals from the whiskers of his moustache. Had Dr. Nagel have needed to comfort himself with the company of polar bears and seals only on Wednesdays, it wouldn't have been that big a problem, but the climate in their bedroom was cooling evening after evening, night after night.

This time, Dr. Nagel wanted to make sure that his wife would be deep asleep. He dissolved a couple of sleeping pills in the pitcher of juice from which he knew his wife would pour herself a drink as soon as she'd come home. Finally, he wrote a short note to his wife that he placed visibly on his nightstand before departing.

After Marianne had wrapped herself in her blanket, Dr. Nagel lay stock still next to her and listened to his wife's even breathing. Silence hummed in the corners of the bedroom. He waited. After four in the morning, it started to rain. Dr. Nagel went to the kitchen to wash the pitcher and glass, so as to leave no evidence. He heard the raindrops patter on the windowsill and was afraid that Marianne would wake up to the sound of the rain. He needn't have worried, his wife was wandering deep in the valley of dreams. The time for action had come.

As Dr. Nagel stepped into the thigh, he felt his palms start to sweat and his heart start to race. It was dark, humid, and warm inside. There was an echo. He could feel a stable pressure in his ears, and the rush of the blood vessels was like the sound of a distant highway, or the buzz of power lines over a field.

Dr. Nagel dug a flashlight out of his backpack. He was standing ankle-deep in red water. It must have been an outlet that carried blood from the heart to the farthest branches of the vascular system. He turned to climb upstream. He was Nagel no longer, but Livingstone. The source of the river was waiting to be found. In the stillness of the tunnel of veins, he could hear screaming monkeys, prattling parrots, roaring lions, and the clatter of the delicate hooves of an antelope herd as it took flight. He observed the world around him through the eyes of a scientist, vigilant and with every sense alert. He was excited by the knowledge that he was walking in a place where no one had trod before, seeing and hearing things that no eye had ever seen and no ear had ever heard.

He made notes, calculations, checked his bearing with a compass. His observations would later enable him to recount his adventure. Walking upstream was arduous, and it was hard to breath. Dr. Nagel soon noticed that he'd dressed too warmly. When the first narrow fork diverged from the river, he stopped to catch his breath and check his coordinates. He sat down on the river bank and took off his cotton shirt, the back and underarms of which were soaked with sweat.

After shoving his shirt in his backpack, Dr. Nagel set off again. He noticed that his eyes had become accustomed to the darkness. He switched off the flashlight, the beam of which had guided his way up to then. The current of the river became stronger. Meanwhile in the other world, in the house on the hill, in a dim bedroom, Marianne woke up to the sound of the telephone.

While the police were rummaging through his house looking for clues, while Marianne and the inspector were making eyes at each other in the kitchen, pondering how to interpret the note, Dr. Nagel was wading in a red stream inside his wife's thigh. His progress had slowed even further and become even harder, as the current had become stronger after Marianne had got up, its force pressing against Dr. Nagel's bare calves. Apart from his backpack and a loincloth made from his pants, he was now naked.

For the first time in his life, Dr. Nagel felt alive—not only as a thinking consciousness, but as muscles, veins, and layers of skin. He was soaked in sweat and felt his muscles, unaccustomed to physical strain, contracting and relaxing, tightening and easing. He felt his lungs gasping for oxygen, his joints creaking and cracking, but submitting to the will of the muscles. The most amazing thing was that he was enjoying it all. It was as if his body, which he had come to consider a necessary evil, a frame thrown together to support the head, had shed its skin in this new environment. He thought that his joy was the joy of a viper slithering in sun at the edge of the forest, with dust and fir needles sticking to its skin, still moist after molting. Or perhaps he was a Celtic shaman, wrapping an eel skin on his arm and feeling the electricity flow through his limb.

On the evening of the 7th of April, the exhausted Dr. Nagel reached his destination. During the nights that he'd spent awake at the weather station, he had chosen for his base camp a location where he'd be able to see two large, collapsed stars for the first time. He knew that they would hang in the dark sky like twin pennies. In the world from which he'd vanished, they weren't stars, but vaccination scars on Marianne's thigh. They reminded Dr. Nagel of their first night together. He had caressed them, kissed them, pressed his loins against them. As he had touched the scars, he had felt years lift from him, and he had laid his palms on Marianne's warm breasts.

When the stars became visible, the scientist took over after the hike. It was time to set up camp. During the next few days, Dr. Nagel didn't spare himself. The first thing he did was carve out a cave in the thickest part of his wife's femur (the pain Marianne felt in her right thigh for a few days was so agonizing that she had to seek comfort in the arms of the police inspector) and decorated it with his few belongings. After that he explored the immediate vicinity of the cave. It appeared safe and suitable for research work. For the most part, the region was a kind of a highland where rocky terrain alternated with patches of grass. There weren't any trees, but in places low, red-leaved bushes fringed the rocky outcroppings.

A river ran through the area. Dr. Nagel didn't need to fear starving to death. As he had made his journey, he had noticed that the river was swarming with fish, which eagerly seized the worms squirming on the end of Dr. Nagel's hooks. There were two types of fish: small red ones and large white ones. The meat of the red ones was nutritious, but left an iron-like aftertaste in his mouth. The white ones had no aftertaste, nor any other taste for that matter. The two species didn't live happily side by side in the currents of the river. The white ones would attack the red ones. Dr. Nagel was amazed by the fury with which they sank their needle-sharp teeth into the scaled sides of the red fish. After the clashes, the mauled corpses of red fish would float on the surface of the river, sometimes just the heads with the rest of the body gnawed away.

Dr. Nagel's life found a rhythm. He began his research, transferring the world onto paper. He had already written his motto on the first page of his notebook before he had set off on his journey: "Dive into the river of doubt time after time. Create in the darkness, only then will you be able to recognize the light." In the dark silence of the thigh, his pen created a world of light and order. Page after page turned into a story. He was like a blind bard, whose lips poured forth the story of the creation of the world, of light and darkness, of the first person.

The story was based on the results of his measurements. Three times a day, Dr. Nagel would pick up the scientific equipment he'd brought with him, survey the weather conditions, and record his findings in his notebook. In between his chores, he fished, read the medical encyclopedia, and went hiking in the rocks, where a morning mist would gather in the hollows. In the evenings he would examine the sky looking for more stars.

Dr. Nagel found himself changing at the same pace as the picture of the world he was studying took shape. He knew that he no longer was the same Dr. Nagel he had been at the beginning of his journey. The muscles of his arms and legs were getting stronger. The skin at the bottom of his feet was thickening from climbing over rocks. His hair, beard, and nails were growing. A month after his arrival, he happened to glimpse his own reflection in the surface of the river and could not believe his eyes: who was that dirty savage with unkempt hair who was lying on his back in the river and looking back at him?

The research soon became dull, as the weather conditions hardly ever fluctuated. It never rained, causing Dr. Nagel to interest himself in changes in temperature. Once he had determined the effect, he became intent on finding the cause. Of particular interest were recurrent heat waves, during which moisture trickled down the walls of the cave and the river surged to the point that it nearly flooded its banks. If he stood at the mouth of the cave and looked across the river during a heat wave, he could see the air ripple over the rocks. The heat waves electrified the air. Dr. Nagel's head would ache. At the end of the third week, he suddenly realized the logic behind the heat waves.

There were two types of heat waves. Sometimes the temperature rose slowly and steadily, at other times the air seemed to become electrified in just a matter of minutes. Dr. Nagel's records revealed that the slow heat waves fell on Wednesdays, which helped him get on the right track. The explanation could be found in the other world. On Wednesdays evenings, Marianne would be standing with legs apart swinging her arms in aerobics class, listening to the rhythmic directions of the aerobics instructor. The more vigorously Marianne would swing her arms and the faster her knees rose and fell and her feet trampled the floor, the hotter the conditions were for her husband, lurking in her thigh.

When Dr. Nagel sought to escape the heat in the cave, when he lay on the bed he'd made from his clothes and fanned his face with a branch from a red-leaved bush, he would be beset by the memory of Marianne. He returned in his thoughts to the world that he had left behind. As if peeping out of the hole he had bored in her thigh, he saw the gym and some twenty women in leotards. The vision titillated Dr. Nagel. He tried to focus his attention on the edge of the ceiling, count floor boards, analyze the pictures hung on the walls of the gym. But his eyes turned time and again to the places where desire and absence became flesh: buttocks, thighs, breasts.

When the workout was over and Marianne stopped jumping, stretching, and dancing, Dr. Nagel sighed with relief. He knew that this was just the calm before the storm, though. He would be tried one more time before the temperature would finally decline: Marianne would hurry to the shower. As the mirrors in the shower disappeared behind a shroud of vapor, the walls of the cave would start dripping with moisture. Dr. Nagel's fingertips tingled as if he'd burned his fingers in the water that was flowing down Marianne's body, trickling onto the floor, and disappearing down the drain. Eyes bloomed on Dr. Nagel's fingertips, and he used them to devour Marianne's body.

Dr. Nagel didn't like the Wednesday heat waves. As he was bathing in perspiration in the solitude of his cave, as if in a vision, he saw himself hunting a pale blue flower that grew on the edge of a spring and touched him with its lustrous leaves. Marianne's face haunted the broad blue circle formed by the flower's petals. It broke his concentration on the truth of numbers, that which can be measured, that which is permanent and certain.

The sudden heat waves, however, were even greater trials. In trying to solve the mystery of them, Dr. Nagel trusted in his intellect, in numbers, and in their uncompromising union. He made calculations, added and subtracted, squared and cubed. Time after time he found himself at a loss. The hardest part was explaining why these heat waves only occurred at night. Dr. Nagel was on the verge of resigning himself to the idea that he'd have to accept the unexplainable as part of the explanation when the answer finally dawned on him. He was fishing on the river bank and became so excited that he dropped his fishing rod in the water and frightened the fish away. The explanation was so obvious, though unpleasant: Dr. Nagel realized that Marianne had taken a lover. Nothing else could explain the sudden nocturnal heat waves. The joy of finding the solution was lessened by the uncertainty of who that mysterious lover was. Who was exciting Marianne to the point that Dr. Nagel nearly broiled to death in his cave?

Dr. Nagel had to resort to using his imagination. Drawing on his jealousy, he concocted a story about Marianne's lover. There were two people in his story: Romeo and Juliet. Romeo was a young broad-shouldered police inspector, who fell head over heels for Juliet's brown eyes while investigating the disappearance of her husband. Night after night he steered his car into the courtyard of Juliet's castle. Swarms of mosquitoes danced in the lights of the castle's lanterns, and the berry bushes at the end of the yard looked like people crouching in the darkness. The drawbridge along which Romeo walked to the gate of the castle bore an uncanny resemblance to concrete tiling. The door that he knocked on looked very much like the door of Dr. Nagel's house. Juliet, whom Romeo embraced, was obviously Marianne's twin sister. Juliet was excited by her lover's kisses. She felt curious fingers lift the hem of her skirt and caress her bare thighs. She succumbed to her lover on the shag rug on the floor of the hall. They made love twice more in the king sized bed in the bedroom. Three times the air inside her thighs was brought to a boil, the blood gushing in hot waves on the walls of the veins. Three times the heat woke up Dr. Nagel, who was bathed in his own sweat.

Life could have gone on like this forever: in two worlds, in two stories. Dr. Nagel would have lived the rest of his days in his cave, knowing that not even death could part him from his unfaithful wife. He would have been able to comfort himself with the thought that they would share the same casket, as they had shared their marriage bed. Marianne would have been able to marry her inspector, give birth to a son and a daughter, and later, when her middle-aged and balding husband ceased to interest her, find a new young lover. No one would remember Dr. Klaus Nagel any longer, the director of that remote weather station, who disappeared one day without a trace.

But their stories intersected one last time. Exactly two years to the day had passed since Dr. Nagel's disappearance. Marianne had spent the weekend at her mother's and was driving home. She was speeding down the night-time freeway. She was tired, her eyelids became heavier and heavier as she stared at the empty road ahead of her.

By the time Marianne saw the elk, it was already too late. Its eyes gleamed in the headlights like diamonds. Marianne should have swerved toward the shoulder of the road to avoid the animal, but she wrenched the wheel in the wrong direction and hit the brakes. It was all over in seconds. The car smashed into the elk, the windshield exploded into thousands of shards, and the glass cut open the animal's side. Marianne had forgotten to put on her seatbelt. She was thrown headlong through the windshield. The car swerved off the road and the carcass of the elk flew off the hood of the car into the undergrowth. A deep silence settled over the desolate road. The car lay on its side, two wheels still spinning. Steam rose from beneath the crumpled hood. Shards of glass were scattered across the road, glimmering in the light of the street lamps. The asphalt was scored by a black skid mark.

Three minutes later a truck happened upon the scene of the accident. The truck driver found three bodies. The woman who had been driving the car had been crushed underneath her vehicle. Shards of glass had mutilated her face. Her right thigh had been severed above the knee. Next to the car sprawled a dead elk. Its stomach had spilled out of the hole in its side. Steam rose from its intestines. The third body lay in front of the car. When the truck driver got closer, he noticed that the man was naked. His skin was covered by a thick layer of grime, his face by a bushy beard. Unkempt hair reached down to his shoulder blades. His nails were four inches long. The trucker shrank back and climbed hastily into his truck. He dialed the emergency number on his car phone.

By the time he put the phone down, other travelers had arrived on the scene. They parked behind the truck and peered down at the accident site from the road above. The truck driver placed warning triangles at either end of the accident site.

The police arrived, as did an ambulance, although the trucker had informed them that there was nothing left but dead bodies. Everyone looked at the naked man with astonishment. Had he been in the woman's car? Why was he naked? The paramedics carried the bodies into the ambulance on stretchers. The accident made the news. The woman was not difficult to identify: the police found her purse inside the car, and in the purse, Marianne Nagel's driver's license. But who was the naked man?

The police started dredging up unsolved missing person's cases. They found a binder, the spine of which was adorned with the name Klaus Nagel. Suspicions arose, but the final identification could be made only after the beard and hair of the deceased had been cut. The identity of the man was confirmed when the shaved face was compared to the picture of Dr. Nagel that had been taken a few weeks before his disappearance. The director of the weather station had been found.

BLUEBERRIES

August emptied his sixth bucket of blueberries into the larger tin tub on the porch of the sauna. He had found a new blueberry patch in a dell about half mile from the house. The depression was nestled between the cliffs surrounding the lake, and it was guarded by two enormous boulders that stood at the foot of the cliff like the unseeing eyes of a giant frog. Blueberry sprigs had sprouted across the hollow in an even carpet, and the sprigs that grew on the sunny southern slope in particular were heavy with blue. August had been crouching in the hollow for two days now, and every time his bucket was full, he went back to his house and emptied the berries into a battered tin tub. The first few buckets were enough to cover the bottom of the tub, and after the fourth load it was almost half full.

August closed the latch on the sauna door and headed back into the woods with his bucket. When he reached the slope again, he sat down to rest in the shadow of the stone giants. He took off his frayed cap, which was blotched with sweat, wiped his forehead dry with his cuff, and licked his dried lips with his tongue. The tranquility of the summer afternoon surrounded him. The sun filtered down through the forest canopy and revealed sprigs here and there as well as spider webs veiling the trees. He rested his eyes on the view of the open lake glimmering between the tree trunks, the sunlight reflected off the water was almost blinding. Suddenly he came to think of winter, the short, cold, and dark days. He saw before his eyes the frozen, snow-covered lake, and reveled in the thought of how he would enjoy the blueberries on a winter morning, how they would bring summer flooding back onto his palate. And how he would enjoy the lingonberries that he would pick next—and the mushrooms that he'd pick after the lingonberries. He looked at the natural world surrounding him, almost overflowing with joy, and grateful that it would provide for him during the coming winter, as it had provided for him the past four winters.

August put his cap back on and grasped the handle of the bucket. He straightened his back. A nasty twinge throbbed between his shoulder blades. Perhaps he had worked too hard that day… little wonder with all the squatting he had been doing. Last night he had fallen into his bed at the end of the day with his back and arms aching and had fallen into sleep like a stone thrown down a well.

He took a couple of steps and glanced around. After propping up the bucket steadily between two tussocks, he cautiously squatted down. He felt a twinge in his back again. August frowned, stripped the blueberries off the nearest sprig, and tossed them into his mouth. It wasn't until he was chewing the berries that he noticed that the tussock the sprig was growing on looked odd. He leaned closer: something pale was peeking out from under the moss. His jaws stopped. He knelt down carefully onto his left knee and used his finger to dig into the ground around the root of the sprig.

It took him a moment to realize that the sprig from which he had taken the blueberries he was chewing was growing out of the left eye socket of a skull that lay on the ground.

August stuck his fingers down his throat. But no matter how much he retched, hacked, and coughed, though he felt his bowels convulse and sweat break out on his forehead, he couldn't make himself vomit, only bitter stomach acids rose into his mouth. He got up and took a deep breath, instinctively looking around. He then knelt down by the tussock and scraped off the rest of the moss covering the skull, growing through the cracks in the bone. Another blueberry sprig was growing in the right eye socket, and a whole clump had sprouted out of its mouth beneath a couple of brown upper teeth. August's mouth felt dry, and the slope seemed suddenly to spin around him, but he grit his teeth and carried on digging. He worked until he had managed to dig out a yellowed human skeleton from amid the sprigs and moss. Decayed rags of clothing covered the ribcage and thigh bones.

August grasped the skull carefully with both hands and lifted it to his eyes. He used his fingers to wipe away the moist grains of sand that clung to the bone. The sun shone through the skull, as there was a hole the size of a bottlecap in the back through which the blueberries had been growing. He lay the skull down on the ground and wiped his forehead dry. From the shore he could hear a sandpiper call as it flew along the water, and suddenly, for a fleeting moment, August saw himself through the bird's eyes: he lay on his back in the shallow water by the shore, his limbs were spread out and his eyes and mouth were open, and a blueberry welled up regularly from his mouth like a blue air bubble.

Four years earlier, August had left his wife, childless, after fifteen years of marriage, resigned his teaching position, and moved into the middle of a vast forest into the old house that he had inherited from his uncle. His friends had thought he'd lost his mind. His divorce didn't come as a surprise to them, at least not to his closest friends, but how could a man who had spent almost his entire life in the city keep himself alive with just a shotgun, fishing nets, and two acres of field? And how would someone who had worked as a teacher for decades adapt to living in the wild, miles from the closest neighbors? Wouldn't the loneliness overwhelm him?

August no longer thought about the anguish he had felt in the beginning, how he would sit for hours on end on the steps of his house wrestling with feelings of guilt with only the peace of the wilderness around him. At first he hadn't heard anything, not even silence, but little by little his ears had grown accustomed to the forest, and the surrounding nature had begun speaking to him. His guilt had also eased with time. Nowadays he was in the habit of sitting in a rocking chair in front of a tall tiled stove with his feet up on a foot stool watching the blaze of the fire through the stove's perforated fireguard. He had cut the ties to his old life in one fell swoop, and no one besides him had been to the house in four years, not one friend or neighbor, not one chance passerby. Not a single pair of eyes had seen August within the walls of his house, seen him fixing his fishing nets, reading, doing the dishes, or playing solitaire by the light of an oil lamp in the evenings. August didn't have any siblings, and his parents were deceased. August had never seen his father, as he had died in war just a few months before the birth of his son. August's mother had often told him how handsome his father had looked in his uniform at the altar. His mother's eyes had always teared up. August soon learned what questions were not allowed: the funeral, the body of his father, which had been shot to pieces.

After his mother's death, August had looked for a place on his bookshelf to put his parent's wedding photo. He wanted to honor that dark-eyed, stern-faced young man, who had stood alone against an overwhelming enemy in the battle that had been his last. Or at least that was what the army messenger who had appeared at their door one morning had told August's mother in an earnest and consolatory voice, while August hung on the hem of her dress.

August visited the grave of his parents a few times a month, whenever he drove his old van the five or so miles to the nearest shop to stock up on food and other supplies. To keep himself from becoming a complete hermit, he'd exchange a couple of words with the people he'd run into, but he never spent more than a few hours in the village.

Soon after moving into the woods, August had started to collect bones. He couldn't remember when or why it had become his hobby, nor did he know where his interest in bones sprung from. Nowadays he no longer saw anything strange about it.

He had found his first bones deep in the woods just a few weeks after his move. A long dead, decomposed hazel grouse had been lying at the base of a spruce. August had picked at the carcass until the last feathers and strips of flesh had come off the bones and then had put the skeleton into his backpack, where he fortunately had had a plastic bag. At home he had spent many hours in the light of the oil lamp cleaning the bones, being careful not to break even the most fragile ones, the needle-thin and dazzlingly beautiful wing bones. In the half-lit hours of an early summer night he had finally succeeded in assembling the delicate lattice of bone. August could still remember the joy that had welled up within him as he admired his creation. He had dabbed small, glossy drops of glue here and there at the most important joints. He was especially taken by the grouse's slender skull, which tapered to a delicate beak in front of its eye sockets.

That same night he had cleared a place for the bone bird on the rough plank shelf in the cellar. Later, when he had found more bones in the woods surrounding the house, he had made more shelves, until they eventually covered every wall in the cellar. Nowadays the cellar was filled with bones from floor to ceiling: There were whole skeletons and individual bones, animal skulls, bone fragments. There were birds, foxes, squirrels, hares; elk bones and bear bones, a deer torso, and a flat-flanked bream.

Not a single human bone had graced August's collection before. As he carried the remains of the unknown person to his house in a black garbage bag, August knew that there wouldn't be enough space for such a large skeleton in his cellar, so he took what he had found to the woodshed. He cleared a space by the wall next to the door and piled the bones on top of empty fertilizer bags like he did with the firewood. He considered putting the skull on top of the pile, but after holding it for some time, he didn't have the heart to leave it in the woodshed, and took it with him inside instead. He found a place for the skull on his bookshelf, between Sophocles' *Oedipus* and Shakespeare's *Hamlet*.

That entire evening, August thought about who the deceased had been, how and why they had died. Every now and again, he glanced at his watch and considered whether or not to inform the local police about his find. He sat in his rocking chair, sank deep into meditation, and wrestled with his conscience for some time. In the end, he decided to keep quiet about it. It appeared that a long time had passed since the death, and he was sure no one was looking the deceased any longer. Why disturb the ashes of a long dead campfire?

August calmed down after he made his decision. He searched through his library, found a dust-covered book on bone finds, and deduced from the size of the skull that the deceased had been a male. The skull's empty sockets and gaping mouth bothered August, and he found himself wondering what color the unknown man's eyes had been, what his eyebrows and face had looked like. Many times during the evening, he though he felt the stranger's gaze on his back and thought that maybe he should have left the skull on top of the pile of bones in the woodshed after all. Maybe a man has a right to his bones even in death.

The next morning, August continued to pick blueberries, because he wanted to get his mind off the deceased. Once the tub was full, he packed the blueberries into boxes and smaller containers and arranged them in impeccable stacks in the freezer chest. He set aside a bowlful to eat right away. Last year he had bought three freezer chests from an auction: one for berries, one for mushrooms, and one for other food supplies. He would need the supplies, because he didn't have a tractor or a snow blower to keep open the narrow road leading to the house, and the only way he could get to the grocery shop in wintertime was to ski.

August was sitting in his rocking chair two days after finding the skeleton when he was overcome by a feeling that he was not alone in the house. He placed his feet onto the floor and listened, but couldn't hear a thing. He got up, walked around the room, pretended to put things in order, watered the plants, walked from window to window. Eventually he gathered the courage to search the house, the upstairs and downstairs and down in the cellar. Don't be foolish, he said to himself as he descended the stairs to the cellar. No one has strayed out here into the sticks for years. In the cellar, he lit the oil lamp and stood in the middle of the floor. In the lamp's quivering light, he looked over his collection and breathed deeply of the faint smell of the bones that his nose had learned to recognize. How beautiful they were! August raised the lamp higher. He moved from shelf to shelf, looking at and caressing his collection. He held the bones in his hands and ran his fingers over their bumps and hollows, their smooth surfaces and sharp edges, and felt himself relax. It was as if some ageless quality of the bones had flowed into him, stopped him in his tracks and calmed him. But as he climbed back upstairs, his anxiety returned. Finally he seized the skull from the bookshelf and took it out to the woodshed. He placed it like a crown on top of the pile of bones and turned its grim face towards the wall. Stare at that, August thought, as he shut the woodshed door and closed the latch.

The following night, August had his first dream in four years. After his divorce, he had stopped having dreams and had accepted the notion that his subconscious was dead, that it was as still and unmoving as a lake in summertime and that nothing stirred the deep waters any longer.

He was still enthralled by the dream in the morning. He woke up soaking with sweat and with a strange metallic taste in his mouth.

He thought that it must have been from the blueberries he had eaten before going to bed, and he gulped down the glass of water he had put by his bedside. The man in the dream had had a familiar face—so familiar, in fact, that August felt he should have recognized him. He must have met that strange man while still living amongst other people. The man had certainly been a sight: he'd had on old-fashioned clothes made out of heavy woolen fabric, and he'd been standing alone on the platform of a strange, red railway station. He'd had a cardboard suitcase at his feet and had been glancing indifferently in the direction from which the train was apparently due to arrive. He was alone on the platform, and the station building also seemed deserted. No one was peering out of its empty windows at the station yard.

In order to shake off the dream, August first opened the window. The light and smells of the summer day came flooding in. The birds bustled in the apple trees in the back yard, and a gentle wind billowed through the thin white curtains. After a breakfast of bread, oatmeal, and blueberries, August hurried down the path to the shore and stepped into his boat, which smelled of tar and which he had loaded with his fishing equipment the night before. He pushed the boat onto the water as he had so many times before and made for the middle of the lake, which was mirror smooth beneath thin, lingering banks of mist. The sun's corona had already climbed over the top of the trees on the nearest island. After rowing a while, August took off his jacket and rolled his sleeves up past his elbows. Then he turned the prow of the boat toward the edge of the reeds where he kept two fish traps. The first one was empty, but as August lifted the other from the water, he could tell by its weight that he'd caught something. He balanced the handle of the pike pole on the edge of the boat and heaved, but the catch was so heavy that he was afraid the boat might tip too far and take on water. Instead he stood up, planted his legs wide, and grabbed the pole with both hands. The fish trap hung on the end of the hook and finally leaped out of the water followed by a shower of glistening beads of water. August saw two muscular pike, their backs sleek and broad, floundering in the trap.

He saw something else as well. When the fish stopped kicking for a moment, his eyes caught a dead pike lying on the bottom of the trap.

Its head had been gnawed bare, and its white jaw bone was shining in the sun. August lost his grip on pole, and the trap fell back into the water with a splash.

After fishing the trap out of the water a second time and slipping the catch into the boat, August marveled at the size of the dead pike. It was almost three feet long, and its bare jaw bone was as big as a fox trap. What a fine addition to his collection! The fish had already started to rot and August could smell the reek as he rowed swiftly toward his home shore. Never before had he come upon such a sight: that pike caught in a fish trap would kill and eat a member of their own species, predators though they were.

When he drew close to the shore, August turned the boat around, because he was in the habit of backing the boat up his jetty. He then thought he saw movement near the corner of the house. He stopped the oars in mid-air. Glimmering drops of water pattered onto the surface of the lake. The oars stuck out like the wing bones, the boat floated in place, and August scanned the shore, but didn't see anything out of the ordinary. Eventually he pushed the blades of the oars back into the water and slowly backed the boat up to the jetty. He kept his eyes on the house and the garden, though. After climbing onto the wooden jetty with the red fish bucket in one hand, he quickened his step. He put the bucket down by the door and dashed to the corner of the house. Nothing, no one. August felt a weight lift off his chest, and was angry at himself for allowing his imagination to run away with him.

In the evening, August heated the sauna. He got some firewood from the shed. The bones were still in their place in a neat stack: shin bones, ribs, wrist bones, thigh bones, hip bones, and ankle bones. Perched atop of the pile was the skull with the hole in the back, staring at the door with empty eyes.

That night, August fell asleep early after drinking half a bottle of home-made cider and eating a handful of fresh blueberries for an evening snack. He had a dream again. A giant pike with handsome, feathered wings floated into view from among the clouds. While flying, it opened and closed its massive maw and clacked its jaws. The creature landed on the top of a spruce, opened its jaws wide, bared its teeth—and began to sing. August, who was standing at the base of the spruce peering up at the strange animal, heard even the birds falling silent to listen. Then, suddenly, the same man appeared in the dream as the night before. He was running in the forest, leaping swiftly over tussocks of blueberry sprigs, weaving through the trees. August could hear the man panting, saw the sweat running down his young face in streams and gluing his hair to his forehead. The man was wearing a uniform, the buttons of his jacket hung open; the front of his undershirt was soaked with sweat. The man stumbled up the gentle slope of a hill, every now and then grabbing the trunk of a pine tree for support. The man didn't appear to see or hear the pike, the giant fish singing away atop the spruce, or August, who was standing silently at the foot of the tree. But August could see that the soldier was afraid, that he was scared for his life every time he glanced back.

August woke up in the morning with the taste of lead in his mouth. He sat up in bed and listened. The silence of the summer night hissed around him. August was certain that something had broken that peace, some noise, just now, a second earlier, and torn him out of the world of his dream. He sat and listened, strained his ears, barely dared to breathe. Then he calmed down, got out of bed, and walked barefoot to the window. It was already light outside, the dark branches of the apple trees were shining, dew-studded harvestmen's webs glistening between them. The lake was calm as a mirror. Veils of mist drifted here and there along the edge of the reeds.

August yawned widely, but didn't go back to bed. When he was weeding the vegetable patch in the afternoon, he found a dead mole. He had always pictured moles as big-boned ploughshares, but there it now lay in the palm of his hand, cold as the handle of a chisel. August raised the mole in front of his face and blew the hairs of the head back, until two black spots were revealed underneath: there were its eyes. He put the mole down and continued to weed. Half an hour later, he had found a bunch of small bones in the soil, and after two hours, he had managed to dig eight mole skeletons out of the vegetable patch. He used a watercolor brush to wipe the bones clean of soil and stacked them on a sheet of newspaper. He skinned the dead mole with a few expert flicks of the knife, and found a place for it amongst the other mole bones. He straightened his back and couldn't help but think that he had planted his vegetables in a mole cemetery. As he gazed at the still lake, he saw himself standing on top of mole catacombs. Tiny vaults delved many feet beneath the ground, side by side and on top of each other. In the depths of each vault, hidden deep in the black soil, gleamed a delicate stack of white bones.

That night, before going to bed, August ate a piece of the blueberry pie he'd baked. He fell asleep as soon as he had lain down and pulled up the blanket. The day spent in the vegetable patch weighed on his limbs, and the last thought that circled in August's mind before sleep took him was that he was getting old.

That night, too, he had a very vivid and very clear dream. The pike was still singing up in the tree, it had piecing mole's eyes, and the gray bark of the spruce smelled of dried resin. The soldier stopped running. He was now crouched at the base of a large boulder with his back to the flank of rock, holding his breath and listening. At that moment August's ears also made out footsteps walking up the slope. He saw the fear in the soldier's eyes, saw the veins bulging in his neck and temples, the teeth worrying his lower lip, his ribs heaving underneath the shirt and woolen coat. As the soldier turned his head towards the approaching steps, something flashed at his neck. His dog tag, August thought, and suddenly realized that it had been the clink of a dog tag against stone that had woken him up the night before. He heard two people approaching, walking up the slope side by side. Right then, the soldier, who had been hiding behind the boulder, leapt up and dashed to the left, toward another giant boulder. August could already see his pursuers, two soldiers with rifles in their hands. He could see the soldiers' uniforms, saw the rank insignia on their collars. One of them dropped down on one knee, raised his gun, and took aim. August didn't hear the shot, but saw the muzzle flare and imagined the bullet flying through the air, until it entered the back of the fugitive's head and threw him on his back on the heather. Just then August cried out: he's one of your own, he yelled, for god's sake don't shoot your own! But in his dream, not a sound escaped his lips. The only sound was the song of the pike, echoing in the canopy high above: there it sang, the mole-eyed pike, clacked its magnificent jaws and silenced the birds.

The next morning August climbed the hill where he had found the skeleton. He kneeled down and leaned forward to examine the spot where the skull had lain. He dug into the cold sand, sifted each handful carefully and piled the sand beside him. After digging for some time, he finally found what he was looking for: a small, flat aluminum tag. It was made to be broken in two, but both sides were intact. August thoroughly wiped the tag clean, rubbing all the sand away. He tried to make out the numbers engraved on the plate, but a few of them were so worn that he couldn't be sure whether they were zeroes or eights.

After hurrying back to the house, August changed into his city clothes, put the tag in the pocket of his worn out leather briefcase, and got in his van. He was gone for two days. When he returned, he parked his van in its usual place in front of the house, went inside, changed his clothes, and came out with a big black garbage bag in his hands. He went directly to the woodshed, put each of the bones he'd found in the woods inside the bag, and then lifted it over his shoulder. Then he made his way into the woods, climbed the hill, found the place where the bones had lain, and kneeled down. For a quarter of an hour, he dug into the gravelly soil with his bare fingers, cupping his hands to lift out the soil and place it to one side. Then he emptied the bag and placed the bones one by one into the pit he'd dug. He balanced the skull on top.

As he squatted there on his knees staring at the punctured skull, August remembered how his steps had echoed on the waxed stone floor in the hall of archives; he remembered the polite, if somewhat surprised, expression of the round-faced archivist when August had introduced himself and handed him the dog tag and said that he'd like to know who it had belonged to.

The archivist had soon recovered from his confusion. When the archivist had asked where August had found the tag, he had had to explain where and when he had found it as accurately as he could. He hadn't mentioned the skeleton, had only said that he had found the tag while berry picking.

"This is the tag of someone who went missing in action," the archivist had said. "It hasn't been broken in two." Then he had said that August should go have some coffee while he looked into the matter. "Come back in an hour."

An hour had been enough. When August returned to the archives, the archivist had been able to tell him who had once carried the tag.

"But...don't you have the same last name?" the archivist had exclaimed after he had told August the name, right after the truth had hit him.

August could no longer remember what he had said to the friendly, unfamiliar person, who had stood in front of him, bewilderment and shock written on his face, holding the aluminium plate that had hung around the neck of August's father in the days of the war. But August did remember that by the time he had reached the street, he had decided never to try to discover who had been buried in his father's grave, the person that his mother's body had been laid to rest beside.

THE AQUARIUM

Lilja slid feet first off the edge of the aquarium and into the water, sunk downwards, and finally thudded onto the bottom of the tank with both feet. Water seemed to dribble into her ears, seep through her tissues, and trickle down into a puddle at the pit of her stomach. The feeling disappeared, however, when she got firm land beneath her feet and found her balance and stood there, amid a silence that she felt as a pressure against her temples. She was surrounded by a green-hued glow that fixed itself onto her skin and the glass sides of the tank. The light of the floor lamp in the living room loomed in the distance. Another, brighter one shone above the aquarium, but it was still dim at the bottom of the tank.

It was hard to move in the water. Lilja had to lean forward and waddle with her legs apart, flexing her stomach muscles, using her arms to help make her way forward. She kicked up sand and small pebbles from the bottom and they whirled around her; the water seemed to become hazier with each step Lilja took. She soon realized that it would be better to swim. She bent her knees, pushed off with her calves, and started vigorously scooping with her arms and kicking with her legs. The plastic aquarium plants swayed to the rhythm of her movements, leaned toward the sides of the aquarium, then back, and away again. It looked as if they were shedding seeds, as the layer of algae that had accumulated on the plastic stems and forks of leaves was shaken loose and twirled away in the water.

Lilja tried to float. She felt the pressure of the water on her neck and armpits, it pressed against her stomach and loins. After a while, she found that it would be best to put her feet on the ground and stand still. The grains of sand and rock began to sink, and the water plants settled down.

She stood still on the bottom of the tank until the water calmed down.

Soon Lilja's eyes happened upon a fish the size of her palm. Its yellow and blue striped head peeked out of a hollow in a plastic rock. Its gills opened and closed, as did its mouth, and its red pectoral fins flapped. It left its hideaway and started to examine this new creature that had appeared in the tank. The fish circled Lilja, and made short, swift sprints past her stomach. It swam, sides quivering, through her field of vision, stopped and stared at Lilja with its bulging eyes, which moved with the same rhythm as its mouth gulped water. All of a sudden, the aquatic dweller would disappear from sight only to reappear again soon to inspect Lilja's back, to nibble the bumps of her spine with its lips. The fish rose past Lilja's shoulder blades to her bare neck, where it tickled her with its pelvic fins, so that she had to shoo it away. Soon it was joined by more fish, large and small, silver flanked and rainbow colored, until most of the inhabitants of the aquarium had worked up the courage to come out of the hiding places where they had sought refuge from her, the intruder.

The first time, Lilja spent twelve minutes in the aquarium.

The next morning, she woke up early and hardly had the patience to get dressed and eat breakfast before hurrying out into the stairwell with a towel tucked under her arm. She heard the elevator move and imagined how one or more people were sitting on the bench of the old-fashioned cage elevator on their way down. Lilja snuck quickly in through her neighbor's door. Just as the elevator rattled past and the floor number painted on the stone floor, three parallel columns, flashed by the elevator passengers' eyes, Lilja locked the dead bolt. She peered through the peephole, but only caught a glimpse of the top of the elevator carriage. As Lilja drew the blinds in her neighbor's living room, she could hear the front door open and close three floors down, and soon, hurried steps clattered on the pavement, multiplied by the echoing courtyard.

It was dark and quiet upstairs in the third floor apartment. Lilja switched on the floor lamp and stood in front of the aquarium. Never before had she seen such a large tank in a private home: it covered the longest wall of the living room, was almost twelve feet high and thirty feet wide, and extended three yards out from the wall. Even so, there were still several yards of space in front of it, as extra space for the aquarium had been appropriated from the bedroom. Walls had been moved, torn down, and rebuilt. In the end, the bedroom had just enough room for a bed.

That was enough, Lilja thought. The bed was enough, it was all they needed.

She looked through the glass into the strange world, which seemed to be cut off from sound. She tilted her head and saw the lamps attached to the ceiling. Their light filtered down into the water from above, but never reached the bottom. She saw the fish, dozens of them, large and small, silver flanked and rainbow colored. Some of them seemed to be sleeping, dreaming on their stomachs at the bottom of the tank or near some of the plastic rocks placed in one of the corners. Others seemed to swim back and forth in the tank, and the hungriest, or the most curious ones, were rooting around the sludge on the bottom.

Lilja fetched the aluminum ladder from the kitchen and put it up in front of the tank. After undressing, she neatly folded her clothes and put them next to her towel on the armrest of the leather couch in the living room. She caught a glimpse of herself in the larger living room mirror and moved so she could see herself fully. "You are beautiful," she said aloud to her reflection with a serious expression, "so very beautiful." Lilja looked at the thirty-something woman standing naked in front of her saying that she was beautiful, so very beautiful.

The rungs of the ladder felt cold against the soles of her feet. Lilja climbed until her head almost touched the ceiling, held the wall and the edge of the tank for support, and maneuvered herself into a sitting position on the edge of the tank. The aquarium wasn't completely full, the water didn't reach all the way to the top. It wouldn't spill over when she slid into the tank.

The water was cool. Lilja took her time getting accustomed to it, splashed her legs in it, her feet shins calves. Then she pushed off, lifted herself up with her arms, held her breath—and dropped forward and down.

That time, on the second day of her neighbor's vacation, she spent an hour in the underwater world.

The next day she lingered there for an hour and a half, and on the fourth day nearly two hours. After getting out of the tank, Lilja would always pad over to her neighbor's bathroom to wash away the slime from the aquarium; it especially seemed to cling to her black tresses and curly pubic hairs. She rummaged through the bathroom cabinet, sniffed the perfumes, fingered the jewelry. Sometimes, before lathering and scrubbing herself clean with a washcloth, Lilja would spray some particularly fine perfume on the back of her hand, hang an extravagant necklace around her neck, and put on makeup—line her eyes with black kohl and paint her lips red—then look at herself in the bathroom mirror and say to her expressionless reflection, "You are ugly, so very ugly." Those times Lilja would always scrub herself more fiercely than usually, so that the cotton washcloth seemed like a grater on her skin; she'd scrub herself until her skin turned red and tingled, red patches appeared on her breasts and thighs, and her loins throbbed. Last of all, she would smear the makeup across her face with her fingers and palms, and then washed it off.

She never cried, though, and by the time she put her clothes back on, she was already so calm and composed that she would get a mop from the cleaning closet in the kitchen and use it to dry her wet foot prints.

Sometimes, Lilja became so calm, that she didn't even notice that, as she was dressing herself, she was being watched by a young, dark-haired woman, who was getting dressing at the same pace as she was. She didn't notice that the woman was smiling at her, that her lips and mouth were moving, slowly and exaggeratedly, and that the words "you are beautiful, so very beautiful" could be read on her lips.

In the evenings, Lilja was like a different person, sitting behind the cash register at the local grocery store, smiling and greeting people and feeding the prices into the register, accepting and handing over money, smiling and saying goodbye and wishing that the evening would come to an end soon and the long, dark night would come.

Morning after morning, Lilja learned to dive into the aquarium more and more carefully, until finally, she raised no sand from the bottom of the aquarium, and the plastic aquatic plants hardly quivered as she sank down to the shadowy bottom, naked, legs held tightly together, arms pressed against her hips, and hair floating in the water.

On the morning of the eighth day, Lilja put on makeup in her neighbor's bathroom before diving into the aquarium. She covered her face with a thick layer of face cream and powder, applied lipstick to her nipples and areolae, and hung a heavy necklace around her neck. When the makeup began to dissolve into the water, when a black trail of mascara flowed from her lashes and the blue on her eyelids faded into the murk, when the lipstick trickled into her mouth and a red wake leeched off her nipples into the water, Lilja thought that, at last, at last something was being released from her. The fish, too, came to wonder at it, gulping water that must have tasted bitter in their mouths.

Lilja spent three hours in the aquarium. For a long time she just sat at the bottom of the tank with her knees pulled up to her chest, arms wrapped around her legs, and stared into the living room through the glass and water. It seemed so far away and unreachable, although it was right there, just inches away, behind the thick glass. The fish swam, dashing and weaving around her, as if she weren't there in their world.

Lilja sat and watched. The pebbles on the floor of the tank left marks on the skin of her buttocks.

After she had stared at the world behind the wall of water for a while, she finally had the courage to see in that room a dark-haired, thirty-something woman, her neighbor, who was admiring herself in the living room mirror, all dressed and made up. She had the courage to see that this woman was going out and was sipping on a glass of white wine she had set on the floor next to the mirror as she was getting ready. The stem of the glass was as tall and thin as the woman picking it up. From the woman's gestures, expressions, and movements, Lilja could see that she was preening herself for a man. "You are beautiful, so very beautiful," Lilja saw her neighbor say aloud to her own reflection.

When Lilja looked even more closely, when she at last dared to see, she could distinguish the man sitting on the living room couch. It was her man sitting there looking at the woman who was getting dressed. And she, the water nymph, knew that, later, the man would take off everything the woman in front of the mirror was now putting on, would undress her slowly, one garment at a time, until the woman would be wearing only the broad necklace; then the man would take her hand and take her to bed, to the bedroom on the other side of the aquarium, where there was only room for a narrow double bed.

That was enough, that was all they needed. The bed was enough.

That evening, when she left her neighbor's apartment, for the first time Lilja didn't feed the fish.

The next morning, she emptied the contents of the bathroom cabinet into the aquarium. Standing on the topmost rung of the ladder, Lilja watched as the lipsticks, powder cases, hair pins and combs, mascara containers, and jars of face cream splashed into the water and disappeared from view. After climbing down the ladder, she saw them again, lying scattered on the bottom of the aquarium. Powder cases looked like clams that had pressed their shells tightly shut, and a mascara wand that had come loose from its container was like a small, black seahorse.

That time, Lilja also left without feeding the fish.

When thirteen days had passed since her neighbor had gone on vacation, the last fish in the aquarium—small and pale and red-eyed—was floating on its back on the surface of the water. Beneath the dead fish, in the sand at the bottom of the aquarium, lay powder and mascara cases, as well as opened tubes of lipstick that the fish had gnawed on in their hunger. The bottom of the tank was glittering differently now than on previous mornings: if she looked closely, if she pressed her face almost against the glass, she could make out very thin, concave and convex shards of glass here and there amid the sand and pebbles.

Lilja had broken all six of the tall-stemmed wine glasses that she had found in the kitchen cupboard and thrown them into the aquarium.

That morning, she was particularly meticulous about her preparations before entering the tank. Her neighbor would be returning home from her vacation after midnight, she had said she would probably be home around two when she had given Lilja her keys. Lilja remembered how her neighbor had rung her doorbell the evening before she left and asked whether Lilja could feed her fish while she was away—two weeks in the sun, a beach holiday with "an absolutely charming new man."

Of course, no problem. She would make sure the fish got what was rightfully theirs. Just like her neighbor got what was rightfully hers.

Lilja remembered them standing in front of the enormous aquarium, remembered her neighbor's instructions about where the fish food was kept and how often she would have to feed them. She was told which of the fish were shy and reclusive, and which were brave and curious. She saw and heard how her neighbor had come to life, how she gleamed and glowed now that she had found "an absolutely charming new man."

He was not a new man. He was an old one, formerly Lilja's. But he did know how to be charming, that she knew and remembered, after all, it hadn't even been three years yet.

She also knew that, after being charming for a time, the man had a habit of leaving. No explanations, no justifications. Just like that..

Lilja stood in front of the mirror and looked into it. You are beautiful, she said. So very beautiful. Not aloud this time, but moving her mouth so that the woman standing in the mirror could read her lips. That thin woman of thirty, the one who looked like her.

That woman, who had shaved her long hair down to a buzz cut.

Lilja pulled on a wig. She adjusted and arranged it for a long time, made sure that it fit tightly and stayed firmly in its place. Then she looked again in the mirror and this time saw her neighbor, a thin woman of thirty. A heavy, silver necklace hung beautifully between her breasts. Lilja saw how fingers caressed the metal, and tilted her head. "You are beautiful, so very beautiful." This time Lilja said it aloud to make sure the other one would hear it. "You are beautiful and desirable, you brought my ex back from the dead. You took him into your bedroom, into your bed behind the aquarium. You have spent the vacation of your life with him. You still don't know who I am. And he doesn't know that I live next door to you and look after your fish."

After Lilja made sure that the chain was not in place, she flicked the lights on in the hall, leaving them on.

As she padded back to the living room, Lilja thought that never again would she be like someone else, never again would she sit behind the cash register in the nearby grocery store, smile and greet people, and feed the prices into the register, never again would she accept and hand over money, smile and say goodbye. Never again would she have to wish that the evening would end and that the long, dark night would come.

The thought comforted her.

The steps of the ladder pressed, cold, against the soles of her feet. Lilja climbed onto the edge of the aquarium and saw the fish floating on their backs on the surface. She stirred the surface of the water enough to send the fish to the other side of the aquarium.

She would no longer have to worry about the water splashing over.

THE PEARL

My name is Jan Stabulas. I am one of the quietest and most inconspicuous workers in our department store, this giant ant-heap swarming with people. No one really pays any attention to me, although I am on display all the time. My job is quite simple: to stand in the menswear department, dressed in fashionable clothes. Now, that doesn't take much, I have heard it said. Well, try it yourself. Try standing for ten hours, without moving, in an awkward, even an unnatural, position, wishing that the air conditioning would work when it was hot, or that it would be switched off when you can feel the draught cutting you to the marrow. Think how the customers stare at you as they pass by, like an object which they cannot buy, and consider your words once more.

My work-area is a low rostrum with a view of the entire second floor. Directly in front of it is the escalator that transports customers from the lower floors, the worlds of food and home textiles. Their faces shine with expectation, excitement glitters on their cheeks as, only halfway to their destination, they rise on tip-toe to see the things that await them on the sales counters. Sometimes the speed of the elevator is not enough for them and, shoving one another and hurling apologies, they leap up the last stairs.

No one ever stops to look at me. Passivity and silence are part of my job. I am a bystander. I do not expect thanks for my work; that is reserved for those who are visible and audible, who take care that things go forward under their own weight. For that reason I was astonished when, a couple of weeks ago, our department head favoured me with her attention. Her name is Therese Wolkers. She is a divorced, middle-aged woman who carries her years with style. She is always pleasant and friendly, and I do not understand why some of my colleagues consider her arrogant and call her names behind her back - Spinster, Hunchback or Mrs Ramrod.

Mrs Wolkers approached me along the corridor between the sales counters. She was shining in the light: energetic and radiant. To her right were the shoes, each of whose steps brought a whiff of adventure, and to her left were men's suits and jackets, without which you cannot be the most desirable man at the party. It was a quiet moment; apart from her, only a couple of people were visible. They looked like the kind of customer who, when a sales assistant approaches, says 'thank you, I'm just looking' and turns to fondle whatever object their fingers encounter in order to avoid having to speak with the salesperson.

Having assisted one of them - an uncertain-looking young man who had enormous cabbage ears (hopefully he was not intending to buy a hat) - Mrs Wolkers glanced around, stepped closer and winked at me! My nose suddenly began to itch, and I almost let a smile escape from my lips. The clothes I had put on that morning in the dressing room, however, demanded a serious expression, and I could not smile. Fortunately, I succeeded in controlling myself. Moving, let alone showing emotion, before the eyes of a department head would have been an unforgivable and amateurish error.

I know that I should not make a mountain out of a molehill: what, after all, could a single wink mean. My colleagues, however, appeared to envy me on its account. They teased me at the end of the day in the shower, said they would fetch the department head to wash my back. I cannot help it: I cannot get the wink of Mrs Wolkers' eye out of my mind. It is as if the fluttering wing of a butterfly has caused a tornado. In two weeks, the blink of an eye has become a treasure, a valuable pearl, which I keep in the jewellery box of my memory and fiddle with in my thoughts. And that pearl speaks to me, whispers and murmurs, makes promises and chatters like a magic ball, and entraps me in the net of its stories.

The rest of the day, after the wink, went slowly. As I sat on my way home in packed bus and stared at the backs of the heads of the passengers sitting in front of me, I was more certain than before that Mrs Wolkers was in love with me. The wink was no doubt a sign, not merely praise or an attempt at encouragement. Perhaps she really was lonely, perhaps she sought someone to protect and comfort her. Why could I not be that person? Naturally, it would not be suitable for me to make the first move, not at work or after work. Jan Stabulas is the quiet kind, the kind that waits.

I had often considered becoming the lover of a mature woman. From an experienced woman I believed I would receive something that has been lacking in my relationships so far: everyday companionship and security. I spent my energy on flirtation and rolling between the sheets; there has been no time for spiritual bonds. I have experienced nothing but beginnings and endings. Nothing in my lovers' beauty, their outer shell, has touched my deeper feelings.

In the rush-hour bus, whose windows withdrew moment by moment into thicker fog, I suddenly realised I was standing on a threshold. The feeling was hazy: I had lost the old order, but had not yet found a new one to replace it. I was Mrs Wolkers' prisoner. Her smiling face, her reddened lips, her slim fingers, flashed before my mind. I could no longer concentrate on familiar things - on reading the newspaper of the passenger in front of me over his shoulder, or wondering whether the back wheels of the articulated bus would rise on to the pavement when the vehicle turned.

After I got off the bus, my legs carried me toward home more lightly than in a long time. At the front door, something strange happened. As I fitted the key into the lock, I felt someone touch me on the shoulder. I started and turned, but there was no one behind me. The courtyard of the terraced building where I stood was deserted. Nothing unusual was to be seen. Three bicycles stood in the bicycle rack, their saddles decorated with caps of snow. A pair of skis and two poles stuck out of the snow, and in my neighbour's doorway a red plastic sledge leaned against the dark green cladding of the wall. The caretaker had gritted the areas by the doors, and among the sand I could make out the brown needles of Christmas trees that had been carried out into the courtyard. When I turned to open the door, I noticed a row of icicles hanging from the eaves: inside every icicle there gleamed a bubble of air, like a gleaming pearl.

In the evening, I saw more new things: tacky rings left by the bottoms of glasses on the kitchen table (I had given a party the previous weekend), the black and greasy dust that had collected on the ventilation grating of the kitchen, the lights on the front panel of the stereo, the transparent skin that remained inside the shell when I broke an egg. As I watched the television that evening, I noticed how dusty the screen was. As I went to bed, I stood, as I always did, in front of the full-length mirror in the living room. With the exception of my cheerfully gaudy boxer shorts, I was naked. There was nothing to complain about in my appearance. Every muscle was as it should be. Often, in the evenings, I imagined that my flat had turned into a studio, and my mirror image was a full-length portrait standing on an easel, depicting an unusually handsome young man. The satisfaction I derived from seeing my body was now mixed for the first time with joy because someone was perhaps interested in me in spite of my handsome appearance.

I cannot deny that I like the vision offered by the mirror when I stand in front of it. I would not have my job, either, without my external attributes. I remember how, both proud and embarrassed, I glued a naked picture of myself to the square reserved for it on the application form. I checked that I had provided all the required information about myself and took the application to the post office the following morning. After a week, I was informed that I had been chosen for the final selection, in which a couple of dozen candidates would participate.

It was then that I saw Mrs Wolkers for the first time. Together with the manager of the department store, she stepped in to the waiting room where we candidates had been directed. We had already been sitting in the room for a quarter of an hour, eying each other warily and waiting impatiently for something to happen. Mrs Wolkers looked confident but friendly. Intelligent eyes peered out from behind her horn-rimmed spectacles. I was surely not the only one who had an effect on her. It was only emphasised by the grey suit, white shirt and pale blue tie of the department-store manager who stood next to her.

The selection process began with formalities. The manager spoke. His monotonous voice emerged from his mouth as if from a tape. Mrs Wolkers did not say a word. We were shaken by the hand and welcomed. The manager asked us to undress, and the first phase of the test began. Twelve candidates were eliminated before the next round. Excitement mounted as we stood, naked, in a row under the expert eyes of the jury. I felt our judges' eyes boring into me, measuring each muscle, each sinew and bone, estimating and evaluating.

I saw some of my competition become embarrassed when Mrs Wolkers stood in front of them. I managed very well. Feeling her gaze on my body, I thought about car engines, clockwork mechanisms, frost batteries and the selection of the football team I supported. Snowshoes and the chemical formula for ice also passed through my mind. Afterwards, some of my fellow competitors said that at that critical moment they had thought about an eight-kilo iron ball, six-inch nails, the structure of the combustion engine or a left-handed backhand at badminton.

After a wait that seemed to last an eternity, those admitted to the next round were selected. To my delight, I found my name on the chosen list. The unlucky ones dressed and left. As they went, they were thanked for their participation. As a memento, they were given badges decorated with the department store's multi-coloured logo.

The relative order of the remaining eight was decided by a practical test. It was simple: we had to take up the position demanded by our future job and hold it for as long as possible. The goal was ten hours; that was, after all, the length of our working day. We were prepared for such a task. I had practised at home in front of the mirror, as had, no doubt, my fellow applicants. Because of the competitive situation and the tension, however, I could not manage the set time, but stopped after eight and a half hours, when a cramp started in my cheek-muscles, which were set in a smile. Nevertheless, I was selected. I was given a bunch of flowers and, with three other fortunate contenders, welcomed to the store.

A couple of months have passed since the selection examination. When I remember it now, after the wink, I recall a couple of swift, isolated glances from Mrs Wolkers. So, maybe? Perhaps her eyes had already picked me out from the crowd. Perhaps Mrs Wolkers was watching me from farther off when a bunch of roses was put into my arms, and imagining that she would soon take the roses' place. Since the wink I have even been reconsidering my move. I have not been working in the menswear department all the time; like the other new arrivals, I began in the display window group. I had to stand in the department store's largest display window, which runs past the wide main street of our city and a pavement swarming with people. At first I was blissfully enthusiastic. I was bursting with self-confidence, motivated and full of energy.

After my very first day at work, I realised why the experienced guard called postings to the display windows polar expeditions. It was winter. There was such a strong draught that the balls of cotton wool which the window-dresser had placed on the floor in imitation of snow jumped around in the narrow space between the window-glass and the velvet curtain. The harsh light of the lamps attached high on the curtain poles dazzled my eyes, and the radiant glow of the lamps made me feel awkward.

I felt as if I were divided in two: icy from the waist down, but bathed in sweat from the waist up. It felt as if I were cowering in the middle of an icy plain, trying not to screw up my eyes in the sun that was reflected off the snow. Veterans of the polar expeditions said they had suffered from snow-blindness and chilblains. They were all afflicted with rheumatism. Some had nightmares in which they were lost on an icefield without food or drink wearing only a bikini or swimming trunks. During my first day at work, I heard the barking of huskies, the slash of a whip and the terrible din of cracks opening up in the ice. I expected to see the sledges of the polar explorers dashing at high speed on the road that opened up before me, horrified people shrinking back from the path of crackling runners, dogs barking and growling, their gums bare, and breath steaming in a cloud around the fur-hooded faces of the men.

Then everything changed. When, one morning, I was making my way toward the window wearing a green ice-suit and a woolly hat, I suddenly felt someone touch my shoulder. Behind me stood Mrs Wolkers. Although it was early in the morning, she was as bright as a lark as she smiled and clicked the nib of a ballpoint pen she held in her hand in and out. 'I have news for you, Stabulas,' she said. Her breath smelled of mint toothpaste. 'You are to be transferred to my department. Menswear, third floor. Congratulations.' Before I had time to digest the information, Mrs Wolkers had ordered me to change out of my ice-suit and into a dark blue, double-breasted suit and had directed me toward the escalator. It was then that I climbed in to this rostrum for the first time.

During my first shift, I enjoyed the warmth as only warmth can be enjoyed. The sudden change of climate played tricks with my imagination. The panting sleigh-dogs and icefields were replaced by sandy beaches and scantily clad women, swaying palms and swinging buttocks. I fell into an erotic trance. I undressed with my eyes the women travelling on the elevator, imagining them stretched into inflammatory positions. When they passed me, I tried to capture their gazes. I remembered a friend who had studied biology remarking, as he held a plump common toad, 'If I ever meet a woman with eyes as beautiful as this creature's, I'll propose immediately.' In the first few days I spent in the menswear department, I was guilty in my thoughts of such proposals five or six times over.

Because I was struggling with my daydreams, it was only after a week that I began to wonder why it was precisely I who should have received the transfer. Perhaps it was a question of simple good fortune; perhaps the choice could have fallen on anyone at all. However, I do not believe in chance. The wink started a jigsaw in my mind. Pieces become visible, and generally, after a few tries, one finds a place for them. I do not bother my head over whether they may possibly also fit in some other place; the most important thing is to fill the gaps. My horror of openings, gaps and holes goes back to my childhood. One summer's day I peered into a neglected well which bored into the ground at the edge of the fallow land behind our house. The well had a rotting plank cover. When I opened it, a stony, slimy coldness poured into my face. The dark gulf smelled of fusty moss. When my eyes had grown used to the darkness, there flashed across the bottom of the well a rat that hid among the ivy that cloaked the pieces of plank and cement rings. That experience has branded me ever since with a longing for order and harmony.

That order has been disturbed by Mrs Wolkers' wink. I no longer peer into the well; I have fallen right down it. I am in the chasm; coldness emanates from the cement rings. I see, and it frightens me. In the evenings, once I get home, I conjure up the jewellery box in which I have placed the wink. I admire the roundness of the pearl. When I stare at it, it feels as if I were dividing in two, as if I were separating from my body, floating in the room and watching myself from the ceiling or on top of the curtain rail. I see beneath me a great eye that opens and closes as rhythmically as a machine. Every time the eye blinks, a pearl rolls out from under it. The giant eyelashes cast their shadow above it, and inside the pearl I can make out a dark shape, a naked person who looks like Mrs Wolkers. When she presses her palm against her hips, it leaves a mark, and when I bend to look, it is the mark of my palm.

A couple of evenings ago I stood in front of the mirror and I noticed that there was something strange about my reflection. It was a moment before I realised what the problem was: my hips had broadened. I took off my boxer shorts to make sure. I could not believe my eyes. Before me stood a man with a woman's hips. The sex organ that hung in the midst of the dark hair looked grotesque and out of place. As I stared at the extraordinary sight, I began to itch, as if biting midges were wandering across my skin.

Shocked, I leaped away from the mirror - and the tickling stopped. I glanced downward, felt my hips with my hand and noticed that the feminine roundness had disappeared. I stepped in front of the mirror: the itching returned, my hips curved. I also realised that my skin had begun to age, to lose its elasticity. I dashed to the wardrobe, took out a sheet and hung it on the mirror to cover it. I sat down on the sofa, sweating, my hands shaking, and stared at the flowery wallpaper of the living room.

I was growing used to the idea. Evening after evening, I undress in front of the mirror and watch Jan Stabulas changing into Therese Wolkers. With the exception of the itching, the metamorphosis is painless. Time after time, I cease to exist and someone else takes my place. The jigsaw pieces find their places without my help. Inside me there grows a pearl that looks like a lidless eye. I have become the prisoner of seeing. I see my hips curve, my breasts well, my muscles retreat from view and my sex organ shrinks and finally disappears among the curly hair.

Today, I bought a wig. Then I bought some lingerie, and asked the assistant to gift-wrap it. They're for a woman whose eyes are as beautiful as yours, I told the assistant. Confused, the woman concentrated, with pink cheeks, on wrapping the ribbon around the paper.

Externally, everything is as it was. I still stand on a rostrum in the menswear section of the department store for ten hours a day. The escalator brings people up from the lower floors, and in their eyes there shines the desire to believe in the stories of the things on sale. I would like to warn them, to urge them to stand on the threshold and think; to choose things they can return if necessary.

No one knows my secret, not even Mrs Wolkers. I still see her every day. It would be wrong to blame her. The wink was a wink, a little flirtation, a friendly gesture. She probably forgot about it straight away; after all, she had more important things to think about. How could she imagine what happens in my flat at night? I succumb because it it is only by succumbing that I can rid myself of temptation. That is why I remove the sheet from the mirror and stare at the echoing well of my core. I gaze at Mrs Therese Wolkers; I gaze at myself. Now I know that this is not a question of division; on the contrary, before the mirror I become whole. My former self was only one half, and what I had believed to be harmony was merely a grand illusion.

My name is Therese Stabulas. I am one of the quietest and most inconspicuous workers in our department store, this giant ant-heap swarming with people. No one really pays any attention to me, although I am on display all the time.

The Garden

When my parents had finished their work in the garden that Friday, the legs of dad's boots and mom's slacks were all covered with pollen. Where the pollen touched skin, it turned into yellowish goo that only smeared when wiped, stuck on their hands, and wouldn't come off even with soap and a scrubbing brush. "There's nothing to do but wait, it'll wear off with time," dad consoled mom at the watering barrel, when there was nothing for it but to give up. Mom looked desperate, shook her head, and looked at her hands, which were red from all the scrubbing.

My parents climbed up to the porch, and mom ducked inside right away. Dad noticed me sitting on a wicker chair at the end of the porch, where I was leafing through a nature book, even though I couldn't read.

"It fell off and split open, Jeremias. Mom and I didn't even have time to get out of the way."

Dad's eyes burned with excitement. Dad's bald patch was splotched with goo, and there were flakes of pollen in the gray curls that framed his scalp. Dad was taking off his boots in the doorway. They weren't cooperating, and wouldn't come off dad's bare, sweaty feet just by him wriggling his leg. Finally he bent over with a grunt and helped them off with his hand. Then he sighed deeply and wiped his hands on his pants, which were already covered with dirt and paint stains.

I crouched in the farthest corner of the porch. The shadow of the ash that grew at the corner of house fell there in the early evening. I lay the book on my lap. Dad was pacing barefoot on the terrace, his thin calves brown and covered with a net of veins. His feet were dirty, and I could see black gunk between his toes, the kind I got sometimes.

"That pod was completely filled with pollen. There was so much of it, several pounds for sure."

I could just barely make out dad's words. He was muttering through the corner of his mouth, which is how I knew that he was upset, that the fruit falling had ruffled him, and mom, too.

I knew the pod he was talking about. Early in the summer, a bulge had appeared on top of a bush that grew at the back of the garden, right on its tallest branch. Over the summer, the small lump swelled into a seed pod, hard as bone. Now, at the end of the summer, and right before it fell off, the pod had grown to the size of a human head and its skin was smooth as eggshell.

We didn't know what the plant was that the fruit was growing on. Though we'd carefully waded through herbariums and books on plants and bothered friends and relatives who knew something about gardening, we hadn't been able to figure out what that bush was. The bush had already been there next to the fence, squatting on a patch of grass bleached by the afternoon sun, when we had bought the house a year ago—yard, garden and all. We hadn't noticed the plant before, because it wasn't particularly impressive or pretty. Its wooden branches were thick as wrists, smooth, and covered with dark bark, and its leaves were the size and shape of hands, and they flapped in the wind, as if they were made of thin sheets of tin.

Because of the sound of its leaves, we named it the tin bush. Later we also started calling it the bulb bush and the pod plant.

Late in the spring, before the bulb appeared, the top branch had for a week been home to a white flower the size of a fist. It had attracted swarms of bees and other nectar-drinking insects. Sometimes the petals were completely covered by insects rummaging around in the mouth of the flower, and we had been afraid that the flower wouldn't be able to carry the weight of all of them and would break off and fall to the ground.

But it held up after all, and when the flower finally withered, that strange bulb appeared in its place.

After that, my parents would sometimes spend their breaks sitting on a bench from where they could keep an eye on the seed pod. I, too, got into the habit of putting a ladder underneath the pod and studying it every day, carefully tapping its dark brown shell with my fingers and running my hand along its surface, which always, even during the most sweltering days, felt cool against my palm. I measured the ball diligently with a measuring tape, until I was able to tell my parents that it was swelling about half an inch a week. They told me that I didn't have to guard it all the time, it wasn't going anywhere, and they shook their heads when I told them I was afraid someone might steal it. It wasn't long before the branch that the seed pod hung from started to bend under the weight of the fruit. The last weeks before the bulb fell off, the branch had been sticking sideways out of the bush looking out of place and a bit funny.

Now the pod lay split open at the base of the bush—and I hadn't seen it fall! I closed my eyes tightly and imagined the four-inch-long stem of the fruit snapping off its base, the branch that had suddenly been freed from the weight of the bulb swinging upwards with a swoosh, and a few seconds later the seed pod hitting the rock surrounded by chickweed with a thump—and splitting open.

Dad slipped inside after mom. I scrambled out of the chair and off the porch. The kitchen window was open, I heard mom clattering the lid of a soup pot. I made my way to the path that led to the back of the garden through beds of perennials. The flower beds were in full bloom. The blazing yellows, reds, and whites weaved a scented veil around themselves. In the haze, bees and flower flies buzzed and butterflies fluttered, perching on flowers only to leap into the air again right away. The grass along the path rose all the way to the backs of my knees, because once something took root in our garden, it was allowed to grow.

A scarecrow was standing askew at the edge of the vegetable patch. Dad and I had hung empty tin cans on its arms, back, and belly. In still weather, the cans didn't clatter. Behind the scarecrow, a belt of shrubs rippled: honeysuckle, dogwoods, and lilac. It was cool underneath the lilacs, and I had often snuck out there to rest on the hottest days. It was still so hot that my sandals stuck to the soles of my feet.

I found quite a mess at the tin bush: the seed pod halves lay on their sides on the ground. One half had rolled to the right side of the rock, the other to the left. There was pollen everywhere: on the husks and the rock, on the grass in a circle many feet wide, on the lower branches of the tin bush. I was careful not to get too close so as not to get myself dirty.

Good thing it's not windy, I thought. If there was the smallest gust of wind, the dust would be everywhere, and it would turn into paste on my sweaty skin.

As evening fell, first mom, and then dad, said they weren't feeling well and went to lie down in bed. "Jeremias," dad said, "we're going to rest for a while. There's some soup left over. It's in the fridge. Have some in the evening if you're hungry. And there's bread in the cupboard."

He closed the bedroom door and I was left all alone. It didn't bother me, I liked being alone. Soon, there wasn't a sound to be heard from the bedroom. I thought that my parents had fallen asleep, because they were sick and tired, but also because they were baffled by the bulb bush having dropped its fruit. Had dad even remembered to cover his head in the afternoon heat? Mom always had to remind him to wear a sun hat.

I let my parents sleep. I went to the watering barrel to skim off the soapy foam that mom and dad had left floating on the surface in net-like tiles on the surface of the water. I sharpened the sickle's blade with the whetstone, so that dad wouldn't have to do it in the morning. For days now, he had been planning on cutting the hay and weeds behind one of the beds of perennials. I wandered around the garden counting raw apples—one finger, one apple—but there were so many that I lost count.

In the end, I settled on just sitting quietly on a bench. I was sure that I could hear the plants growing: their roots rustling in the darkness of soil, earthworms munching their narrow tunnels into the earth, and moles snuffling in their nests beneath the vegetable patch. Dad had told me about the life of a garden, about what happens in nature.

At eight in the evening, I got hungry. In the kitchen, I ate cold vegetable soup and sweet sourdough bread made with sunflower seeds and malt. For dessert I found some yoghurt that mom had made in the fridge.

I still couldn't hear anything through the closed bedroom door. The whole house was very quiet, only the fridge whirred from time to time. A small bird chirped for a short while out in the garden, right under an open window. When I got to the window, the bird had already flown further away. I could now hear its nervous voice behind the hedge, coming from the shelter of the foliage.

After I'd eaten, I sat on the porch for a while and leafed through the book that I still hadn't finished. There was a big, red picture of a sunset. As I looked at it and stroked the page with my fingers, I noticed that the sun actually was setting, bathing the crowns of the trees in crimson before dropping down behind them. It was the lightless moment before dusk. The time of shadows, I thought as I glanced around furtively. The ground began to cool, the night pressed dew onto the grass and fanned the scent of soil and moldering plants. The buzz of insects had already ceased, and the sounds of birds could no longer be heard either.

I held out on the porch for almost two hours. At half past ten it was already too dim to do anything outside, and I got goose bumps on the skin of my bare arms. I slipped a bookmark between the pages, closed the book, went inside, and knocked on my parent's bedroom door. No answer. I knocked again, a little louder. No answer. I turned the handle and carefully pushed the door open.

Although it was dark in the room, I could see right away that mom and dad were still sleeping. They were resting side by side on their backs, dad on the right and mom on the left, and they were holding hands. They were still wearing their gardening clothes. The stains of pollen stood out as dark patches on the fabric. Dad's mouth was open, as it always was when he was in a deep sleep.

I tiptoed out and closed the door behind me.

It wasn't until I got to my room upstairs and slipped under the covers that it occurred to me that dad hadn't been snoring. He always snored when he slept on his back.

Mom and dad didn't get out of bed the next day, or the day after that. The sickness seemed to have sapped the last shreds of their strength. Every time I peeked inside the bedroom, they were resting on their backs, holding hands, with serene faces. I was certain that when I wasn't there to see it, they were smiling at each other, and that gave them strength to fight the sickness.

I took care of them as best I could. In the morning I would open the bedroom blinds and open the window a bit to let in the fresh air.

They needed light, that I knew. Sunlight and fresh air. The light that seeped in through the narrow gaps in the blinds made the room stripy. My parents look quite strange, pallid, blotchy, and stripy. Now and then it even seemed as if the color of the pollen stains had deepened, that edges of the stains had spread out. Sometimes, as if with their last strength, without opening their eyes, mom and dad tried to talk to me: their eyelids quivered and the corners of their mouths twitched, and if I leaned down close to them, I could hear fragmented words: …food for you, Jeremias…don't worry…this will…pass…water…the garden…

Twice a day, at one in the afternoon and at six in the evening, I stacked food on a tray and carried it to my parent's room. I had cleared off the nightstand. Luckily I knew how to boil potatoes and fry the bits of meat that mom had stocked the freezer with during the winter. I picked salad, onions, and cabbage from the vegetable patch. There was also bread in the freezer, the good wholegrain bread that mom baked. Whatever else I needed, I got from the store: mom kept the food money in a coffee can in the back of the pantry.

But mom and dad were in such bad shape that they had no appetite. I tried to persuade them to eat, but it didn't help. Their meals stood untouched, and stacks of trays started to pile up in the room. After a couple of days, clouds of shiny black flies burst into the air from the piles of dishes, and after buzzing in the air for a while, landed in different places all around the room: near the ceiling, on the wall, on the lampshade, on plates, on the edge of a glass of juice. The boldest of them even used my parents' foreheads or bellies as runways.

The flies soon got used to me and didn't get scared off. They were so fascinated by the food, so hungry, that I could get a close look as they tugged on pieces of meat or salad with their long mouths. Every once in a while, they would groom their legs or shake their wings.

Since mom and dad didn't seem bothered by the flies, I let them be. God's innocent creations, mom would say. Dad thought that mom was too gentle.

I had tucked mom and dad in under a woolen blanket, which usually hung over the back of the couch in the living room. I thought they might be cold, because they had felt cold when I had touched their foreheads a few days earlier. As they didn't complain about the smell coming from the leftovers that clung to the room, I started to close the window for the night, so that they wouldn't catch any more of a cold.

During the daytime, I worked in the garden. There was plenty of work, maybe even too much for just one person, but I did everything I could. Luckily, dad had taught me. I watered and weeded, cut the grass, and used the sickle on the hay behind the bed of perennials like dad had talked about before he got sick. After a while, I began to build a fence around the compost. Actually I just picked up where dad had left off, as he had already put up most of the posts. I hammered rails between the posts and then nailed planks upright onto the rails, leaving an inch between them. I didn't get the planks completely straight, but I thought the fence turned out pretty good just the same. I was disappointed, though, that dad didn't have the strength to get up and take a look at it.

In the evenings I often sat in my parents' room and told them all the things I'd done in the garden. I knew how important the garden was to them and how they enjoyed hearing about my chores and that I was taking care of things now that they were bedridden. I tried to tell them everything as best I could, putting my heart into it and gesturing with my hands. I told them about the chirping crickets, the frogs splashing around in the small pond, and the birds that would stop by for a drink. I told them about the leopard plant's yellow flowers and about how I'd snipped away the dried leaves and the stems of the blossoms that had already withered in the perennial bed. How I'd sawed the fence planks in the backyard on the sawbuck that dad had made, and how saw dust had piled up next to the buck, under the spot where I used the saw. I told them how handy I had been with the hammer, how neatly the nails had sunk into the rails of the fence. I described the mosquitoes that swarmed above the water barrel in the evening in the light of the setting sun.

What I didn't tell them was how many times I had hit my finger with the hammer, that the thumb and middle finger of my left hand ached and the fingernails had turned black.

Mom and dad listened to my stories in silence with their eyes closed.

I understood that they didn't want to waste their energy on talking, but I still wished that they would have thanked me for my hard work and that mom would have caressed my hair or cheek. One time I whispered in my mom's ear that I missed them, but she didn't open her eyes, just kept on sleeping. I started to feel a bit shy.

It was sweet how, day in day out, they kept holding hands without being ashamed, even though I could see. And I was so happy when, sometimes, I thought I saw one of them nod their head at me approvingly.

One day, a new plant had grown at the foot of the pod bush. A deep green sprout, four inches tall, had pushed up in the middle of the seed pod halves and the grass and the pollen plastered on the ground. I put down my watering can and bent down to examine the newcomer: would we be getting a new tin bush? I ran to tell mom and dad straight away.

The next day I found another sprout next to the first one. Then a third, and so on until the bush was surrounded by a circle of strong, fast-growing sprouts that buried the seed pod halves beneath them.

When the phone started ringing, it almost scared me to death. It was evening and dark. I was lying in my bed hugging my teddy bear when that insistent, disturbing sound reached my ears. I sat up. I thought that a racket like that would wake the dead in their graves, as mom would sometimes say. When the noise just wouldn't quit, I got out of bed and crept down the stairs in my t-shirt. Step after step the ringing got louder, more metallic, more insistent.

It had surely woken up mom and dad.

It felt as if the entire house was throbbing in time with the repetitive ringing, as if there was a gigantic, chiming metal heart somewhere deep inside the building. I was about to pick up the receiver when the noise stopped. I stood in the deserted hallway with my arm stretched out, certain that whoever had been calling would soon try again. That beautiful, black object attached to the wall at the height of my eyes kept silent, however.

After I peeked inside my parents' bedroom, I pulled the telephone cord out of the socket.

It was lucky my parents hadn't been woken up by the ringing. And it wouldn't ever wake them up, I thought, as the plug clattered onto the floor. I made sure that the front door was locked and all the windows were closed. As I climbed back upstairs, my ears were still haunted by that metallic noise. It clanged in the walls of the hall and deepened the darkness in the corners.

I lay in bed and waited for sleep to come. I decided that I would no longer bring food to my parents. They weren't eating, and the room was already full of trays, dishes, and cutlery. I didn't have time to clear them up, because I had to tend the garden, though it would be good for them to have food when they woke up. They'd be hungry for sure.

The next morning, the smell has become so strong that I could taste it. The flies seemed to have multiplied even more, and white, lively larvae were grazing in the mold on the sides of some of the chunks of meat.

I still had to go to the room, and regularly at that, since I had to take care of the watering. Everything that grows needs moisture, as mom used to say. Water is the alpha and omega, the elixir of life.

I water the strong, deep green sprouts growing in dad's head, in the middle of his bald spot. Mom's right palm is also looking promisingly green, as are both of their clothes.

The pollen stains shed a moss-like fluff onto the floor, and the fluff has grown ever so thin roots through the fabric. The roots are attached to my parents' skin and if I bend down close enough, I can see that the roots have spread their webs underneath their skin. Their veins have become so pale that they're completely invisible.

I water them four times a week. At the same time I pick up the bits that have fallen off. One of mom's ears plunked onto the floor yesterday, and dad's left arm, which for the longest time was hanging over the edge of the bed, has now fallen clean off. There is a hollow in his shoulder, where the shoulder joint used to be. At the bottom of the hollow, I can see some green sprouting. I wrapped it carefully in a clean piece of cloth after I shooed away the flies.

Last spring, we covered the vegetable patch with gauze, and now it's thriving!

Some evenings, I still spend time with mom and dad, because I know that it's important to them. I tell them how well everything is growing in the garden and what a handsome grove of seedlings has spread out around the tin bush where the seed pod once fell. I describe the shoots that are now over nine feet tall and the white flowers that have appeared on top of them. Whenever I compliment dad on the nearly three-foot-tall bulb bush growing out of his forehead, he always looks pleased.

I'm certain that mom squeezes his hand with pride then. I'm certain that the knowledge gives them joy and comforts them and that it's helping them get better. Maybe already tomorrow they'll get out of bed and continue what's most important in the world: nurturing new life.

THE LIBRARY

1

When the lights go out, Marlies is sitting in the third-floor restroom of the library. There is a small snap, the fluorescent light on the ceiling stops humming, and everything becomes quiet and dark.

At first she thinks that someone must have hit the light switch by accident or as a prank, as the switch is on the outside by the doorframe. Then she remembers that the hallway had seemed so quiet and forgotten that it's unlikely that anyone would have found their way here.

When she slipped into the restroom, Marlies had wondered why it had been built in such a remote corner of the building. Maybe for the cleaners, seeing as it was next to a cleaning closet. She'd peeked inside the closet, seen the mops and brooms hanging on hooks on the walls, the detergent bottles and cleaning rags lying on the shelf. The dust bunnies by the wall had moved when she had opened the door.

The fuse must have blown, Marlies reassures herself in the darkness. She gets up off the toilet and flushes it. As she lets go of the chain, Marlies can hear the water gurgling and gushing into the bowl and closes the lid to prevent water from splashing on her bare legs.

The darkness hums around her. The only sound is the quiet gurgling and dribbling of the toilet as the water tank starts to fill up.

She bends her knees carefully so as not to hit her head on the door, and tugs her pantyhose and jeans up. On their way up, they catch on the edge of the wooden seat, which rises a couple of inches and then slams back down, startling her. The restroom doesn't have a basin or a faucet, just the toilet bowl. At least there's paper, Marlies thinks, wiping her hand on a square of paper she tears off the roll of toilet paper and tossing it in the direction of the garbage can nestled in the corner. She pricks up her ears, trying to hear whether the paper hits the can or the floor.

Marlies turns the handle and opens the door: the lights are off in the hallway as well. Luckily, there are two windows about six feet away on the wall to the left, and they provide enough light for her to fumble her way forward. The window panes are made of glass reinforced with a dense mesh of corrugated wire.

Strange how it's always so quiet in the dark, she thinks. Even small sounds seem loud. Maybe it wasn't such a good idea to come to such a remote hallway, but all of the library's public bathrooms were occupied, and the need hit so suddenly and was so urgent: the stomach bug had left her with a runny stomach, though she could keep her food down now. She'd take a warm bath when she'd get home, soak in the tub for at least an hour. Hot water might calm down her stomach as well.

Marlies feels her way along the wall. The windows and the light they let in are already behind her. A few more steps will bring her to the third floor landing where she will see the rows of bookshelves along the walls on the left and on the right. The library's main stairs will be in front of her, and she can follow them down to the second floor and the ground floor, where the check-out desks are located.

At least there the green emergency lights will be on, if nothing else. And maybe the librarians or the janitors will have flashlights, or even candles, stashed in the bottom of some drawer or locker. How beautiful the library hall would look, lit by dozens of candles: the old, oak shelves and tables and chairs and the books, tens of thousands of books waiting for their readers on the bookshelves. The lights of the city would shine through the windows in the lobby. Large snowflakes, like white rags, would float down from the sky into the halo of the streetlights.

A scene fit for a postcard.

The third floor landing is also completely dark, with only the emergency exit signs shining their green light above the doors. As she steps through the door, Marlies expects light, but something else, as well. It takes a moment before she realizes what: sound. She had expected to hear sounds, the normal sounds of the library: footsteps tramping on the stone floor, soft-spoken, whispered conversations, the ringing of the staff's phones.

But there is no sound, the silence is as deep as a well.

Marlies walks to the top of the stairs and peers over the railing. Her eyes are already getting used to the darkness, but she still can't see anyone down on the second floor. She instinctively takes a look at her watch: it isn't closing time yet. She had been in the bathroom ten minutes at most, and the clock on the reading room wall had shown eight minutes to six when she had rushed out to look for a toilet.

Marlies doesn't take the stairs down, but turns and heads to the left instead. The third floor is a wide mezzanine above the floors below and is home to reference works and non-fiction. Information pressed between covers, a few desks and chairs. She walks past the nearest desk, which is covered with open books. There is a half empty plastic water bottle and a couple of CD cases next to one of the books. One of the cases is open, the CD missing.

She is certain that when she had climbed up the stairs, she had seen a young, ponytailed girl wearing earphones hunched over a book. And hadn't there been someone sitting next to the girl—where a dictionary now lay open? Some older person, an adult?

Marlies walks around the entire third floor mezzanine without seeing anyone. She does find signs of other people, though. Another desk also has things lying on it, a pencil case full of pens and a notebook, its grid-lined pages covered in a young person's handwriting—geographical facts copied from the book lying next to the notebook. Here and there, a trace of perfume wafts through the air between the shelves. The floor is speckled by wet shoe prints, gravel tracked inside on the soles of shoes crunches under her feet.

Marlies descends one floor, but finds no one there, either.

Once all the way down, she rests at the foot of the stairs and peers up. In the dimness she can make out the familiar architectural details of the library, the hundred-year-old features of the venerable and well-kept building that she likes so much. The ground floor is a bit better lit than the upper floors, as two bright street lamps stand outside in the courtyard, and the lobby window lets some of their light seep in. A snow drift almost three feet high has piled up along the courtyard walls, and more is falling gently from the sky.

Everything is as it should be, Marlies thinks. Except that there are no lights. And all the people have disappeared.

2

Marlies had found some food in the staff room fridge: yogurt and sandwiches with lettuce, eggs, and tuna. She'd also found milk and juice, one carton each. She'd poured the milk down the drain, because it had smelled dubious and she didn't want to take the risk with her stomach still acting up. She had also opened the freezer chest, but after feeling around inside, found it to be empty.

Marlies only ever eats a little. Only enough to satisfy the worst hunger. She doesn't dare to think what will happen when the food runs out. She'll be rescued before that for sure.

She has spent the past two days going over the entire library, searching and exploring, snooping and rummaging. She has taken a peek to at least see what's behind all the unlocked doors. Now, over two days after the lights went off, Marlies has a clear picture of the situation. She sits on the old leather couch of the staff room. All the food that she was able to find in the library is in this room, either in the fridge, which is slowly warming up, or in the cupboards in the kitchenette. Fortunately she'd found two grocery bags in the entrance hall coat check. They were sitting on the shoe rack, concealed under the hems of coats. She found pasta, cans of preserves, bread, mineral water, milk and juice, as well as six bottles of beer. Luckily there's still water coming from the tap, at least for the time being. At the back of a cupboard she found some dry goods—crackers, tea, coffee, raisins, rice cakes, and an almost empty bag of refined sugar. There are no pots or other proper cooking utensils, but she'll make do, at least for a while.

There still is no electricity, and the emergency exit lights had gone out the day before as well. Phones aren't working, not the library's landlines nor any cell phones. In addition to trying her own cell phone, Marlies had tried two others. One she found in the pocket of one of the overcoats in the entrance hall, the other on the desk in the library manager's office. The phones were dead and didn't even ring when she dialed the emergency number over and over again before trying to call home one more time.

When the freezer chest had begun to melt, she had emptied the paper towel dispenser in the nearest bathroom and stuffed the towels into the compartment. Not much water leaked onto the floor.

Marlies has spent the nights in the staff room after having cobbled together a primitive bed from coats and chair cushions. Her eyes have already grown accustomed to the darkness or half-light, but not to the sight visible through the library's windows: a transparent wall has appeared around the building. Marlies doesn't know whether the wall is made of glass or plastic or fiberglass or something entirely else, but she assumes it's glass, because she can see through it so well. The existence of the wall is easy to miss unless one happens to lift one's gaze to the height of about nine feet, where the top edge of the barrier can be seen against the neighboring building.

There seems to be no opening of any kind on the wall.

Marlies realizes that the wall had been there already on the first night, when she frantically tried to escape the library.

At first she'd thought that the door had some kind of electric lock, which of course wasn't working. But the lock had had a mechanical latch, which had turned. Even so, the door hadn't opened—no matter how much she pushed, even when she put down her purse and strained against the door with both hands, yelling and cursing.

The following morning, at day break, Marlies had seen the wall. It wasn't thick, perhaps only an inch or so, but it looked sturdy. Nine feet high, it—as she later noticed—enclosed the entire library. It was flush to the wall, following the shapes of the building, its curves and corners, its nooks and ledges.

No one could get into the library, or out of it.

But who would try to get in? All life seemed to have vanished from the world outside the library. Not a single living creature caught Marlies' eye, even though she had dashed from window to window to stare outside.

Only the sky is moving, falling in the form of snowflakes for the third day in row already. The snow banks are growing, already reaching up to the height of Marlies' chest right behind the glass wall. She watches how the cars parked on the street are slowly being buried under the snow, how the snow is piling up on the roofs and balcony railings of buildings, on the streets and tree branches.

On the third day, Marlies batters the large window in the lobby with the legs of a metal chair. The first hit leaves only a small scratch on the window, but when she strikes the glass again, cracks start to radiate out from the scratch. On the sixth strike, the window shatters and falls to the floor in sheets of broken glass.

The chair doesn't make a mark of any kind on the transparent wall, which Marlies is now able to touch through the broken window. Not even when she hits it as hard as she can, swings the chair in a wide arc and lets the metal legs smash into the wall so hard that it hurts her shoulders, and the chair flies from her hands.

Not one scratch.

Marlies tries one more time. She gets the metal coat rack from the entrance hall and manages to throw it base first against the wall. But the coat rack is so heavy—Marlies is only barely able to lift it—and she can't get any power behind the throw.

Not one scratch.

3

Marlies makes herself as comfortable as possible in the staff room. She had been happy to find matches, a bunch of tea lights, and four candles in a drawer next to the sink. She only ever lights one tea light at a time and only burns it for half an hour. She resorts to the candles only when she goes walking around the library, wandering back and forth between the shelves, or roams the deserted hallways. She tries not to think about her family, her husband and two children, who had surely been waiting for her to come home the night she became a prisoner; after all, she had only meant to make a quick stop at the library and then hurry home for dinner. She and her husband always made dinner together. The children would be underfoot, nagging them for bits of chopped vegetables or mushrooms, or whatever else happened to be on the chopping board. Marlies tries to banish the thought of her two daughters, their despair at the disappearance of their mother, their expressions and gestures, their voices and scents, but every now and again she drops her guard, and some memory slips through and brings tears to her eyes.

Then she reassures herself that soon everything will be back to normal, and she will see her loved ones again.

When six days have passed since the appearance of the wall, Marlies inventories her food supplies with concern: even if she were to eat only enough to stay alive, the food would only last a week. As soon as this sinks in, Marlies smothers the anxiety that has crept into her mind and tells herself that something will surely happen before that. She doesn't dare to think what that might be, but just the thought of change is comforting. There must be life outside; it is clear that, any time now, someone will realize and come look for her in the library.

To keep her fear in check, Marlies tries to delve into other worlds: at least she isn't in any danger of running out of books to read. On the best days, she reads seven hours a day, nearly all of the daylight hours. The best light is in front of the big windows in the lobby, where she's moved a comfortable chair. Usually she lifts her legs up on another chair and wraps one of the overcoats from the coat rack around them for warmth. From here she is also able to keep an eye on the yard in case someone comes looking for her, or comes knocking on the wall at the main entrance for some other reason.

But who would that be? Her husband...and daughters? The police? The army? Her colleagues?

On the night between the sixth and seventh day, Marlies sleeps only a few hours. She is scared, and the more scared she gets, the more she misses her family. In the middle of the night she gets up, turns on her cell phone, and dials her husband's number. Everything is as it should be on the screen of her phone, and tears rise to Marlies' eyes. But the call won't connect, not even though she tries it again and again. Even the emergency number remains dead. After she's been up shivering for almost an hour and has tried every number in her phone book several times, Marlies gives up and turns off the phone, to keep the battery from dying.

It's no use trying to sleep. The clock on the wall shows a quarter to four. She gets dressed, digs a candle out of the drawer, puts it on a saucer, and strikes a match to light the wick.

Unbelievable silence.

Marlies sneaks down the hallway in her socks as quietly as she can, as she has begun to dread all sounds, even the most common ones. Slowly she ascends the stairs to the third floor, sheltering the flickering flame with her left hand. Climbing the stairs makes her pant. She feels weak, her stomach has become hollow and shrunken from the lack of food. On the third floor, she stops and looks down, then wanders a while around the mezzanine, and looks at the things lying on the desks.

Everything is as it was back then, on the first evening, when the lights went out. Marlies has been careful not to touch anything that people have left behind. She is certain that tampering with them would be bad luck.

Then Marlies hears a sound.

She doesn't notice it right away. It doesn't get her attention until she hears it—or imagines hearing it—a second time. The hand holding the saucer and the candle begins to tremble. Marlies holds her breath. A gushing sound is coming from somewhere far off. She swallows and looks around. No one is at the main entrance downstairs. Certainly there is no one in the downstairs lobby. There is no one else on the third floor but her, of that she is sure.

Is the sound coming from the second floor?

She can make out the sound again, but can't pin down where it's coming from. Is she imagining it? Is she losing her mind, hearing things? Marlies takes a couple of tentative steps. In front of her is a brown wooden door, and she knows what's behind it: a hallway, two windows along the wall on the right, a cleaning closet and a bathroom at the end. Dark and echoing.

She is just about to press her ear against the hallway door, when she hears the sound again. She moves the candle to her left hand and turns the handle with her right. The door opens slightly, the flame of the candle flickers in a gust of air, almost dies out.

Marlies slips through the door into the hallway. She makes her way forward in the light of the candle. She passes the windows and their faint light to her right. The cold of the stone floor seeps through her socks into the soles of her feet.

She can still hear the gushing. Now Marlies recognizes it. With her heart pounding she takes a final few steps and sweeps the bathroom door open. The movement blows out the candle, the wick is left smoking.

Marlies crouches down. She feels the floor with her hand and places the saucer with the candle down in the doorway. She doesn't bother trying the light switch. In the pitch dark, she gropes around with her hands, turns and squeezes into the confined stall.

Up near the ceiling, the water is gurgling in its enamel tank, but no longer gushing into the toilet bowl.

Marlies opens the buttons of her jeans, pulls them and her pantyhose down, and takes a seat.

The moment her bare thighs hit the seat, the fluorescent light flickers. At first it flashes, once, then buzzes—then the light flares along the entire length of the tube. Marlies blinks and uses her hands to shelter her eyes from the piercing light. She stands up, pulls up her jeans, and again the seat slams down by accident.

Then she leaps out of the bathroom: the entire hallway is bathed in light!

Marlies feels as if electricity is coursing through her body. She hurries to the end of the hallway and out the door. In the library, people turn to look at the half-dressed woman leaping down the stairs several steps at a time, without stopping, first from the third floor to the second, then to the ground floor. Some are even quick enough to notice that she isn't wearing any shoes.

She doesn't even stop at the big windows in the lobby, where the janitor and a group of curious people stand wondering at the smashed window, but charges straight to the main entrance and throws the door wide in front of her.

Behind the door she falls, almost throws herself, into the arms of the people coming to the library.

THE REFRIGERATOR

The first time I heard about Ahab was three weeks after I had started working as a bus driver for the city's transport service. It was a Monday, a typical boring Monday, and the day was already half gone. I had just come to the break room and was standing by the counter ordering a coffee and a danish, when I half-heard the drivers at a nearby table talking about something, visibly excited and gesturing with their hands. I loaded my snack onto a tray and made my way toward them. I was interested in what could have made my usually steady and taciturn colleagues so animated and lively. When I approached the table, however, the buzz of conversation died down quickly, as if according to some unspoken agreement. I noticed how some of the drivers furtively exchanged meaningful glances. I didn't want to be so paranoid as to think that they had been talking about me, even though I knew that they were cautious and had their suspicions about me. After all, I was the first foreign bus driver in this small town, and for many of them their first colleague to speak the language haltingly and with a strange lilt.

Everyone was polite, though. They made room for me at the table, someone took a chair from the empty table next to us, and gestured for me to sit. I looked them bravely in the eye and nodded a greeting. A palpable silence descended for a moment around the table. I couldn't help but think that they had been bad-mouthing me after all, so I was prepared for the worst when Flask, a driver close to retirement who was known to be a conscientious and serious man and a father-figure to us younger drivers, finally broke the silence and said:

"Ishmael, guess what we were just talking about."

"What? I don't know, football?"

Flask shook his head with a stern look on his face.

"We were talking about Ahab, Ishmael."

I sipped my coffee and took a furtive glance at the people sitting at the table. No one was grinning or making any other faces.

"Ahab? Who is he?"

"Ahab rides line 15 from one end to the other," broke in Stubb, a half-bald hulk of a man, who had served in the city's transport services "since time immemorial," as he would say.

"Ah, a new driver!" I exclaimed.

Everyone around the table burst into laughter.

"No, Ismael, Ahab is not a driver. Ahab is a passenger!" Flask corrected me with a smile on his face.

"I haven't yet driven number 15. But tomorrow. Tomorrow I will drive."

Flask's face lit up even more, and a twinkle lit up in his eyes. I decided to be careful.

"You'll be driving number 15 tomorrow, eh?" Flask shot a triumphant look at the others. His mouth broadened into a grin, and he patted my shoulder with his wide mitt. "Then you'll meet Ahab, Ishmael. Ahab takes the number 15 bus every day. Day in, day out."

I didn't know what "day in, day out" meant, but I decided to flash a broad smile and take a sip from my coffee. I thought that they had some scheme in mind for me. I had heard that in many workplaces, new employees had to go through some strange rite. Maybe Ahab was my rite. I decided to try to fish out more information about this mysterious man.

"Is there something unusual about Ahab, then?"

Again my colleagues exchanged meaningful glances. Flask acted as the spokesman again.

"Something unusual? No, nothing at all. The unusual thing about Ahab is that there is absolutely nothing unusual about him. The most common middle-aged man you've ever seen, a small, dried-up geezer, who wears an ulster that's so big on him it looks like he could get lost in it. Nose like a hawk and eyes like two black cinders."

The others nodded solemnly, one of them shook his head, lost in his own thoughts.

"Then why are you spending so much time talking about him?" I asked and took a big bite out of my danish. The jam was sickly sweet and sticky, and it made my teeth ache.

"Because he always just appears in the bus out of thin air. Like this morning. And I can guarantee that he didn't come in through the front door like the rest of the passengers or through the middle doors. But there he was, sitting in the back seat. I noticed him this morning a bit after eight."

A heavy silence fell after Flask's words. I wondered for a while whether they expected me to break it.

"A passenger traveling without a valid ticket should be shown out of the vehicle politely but without delay," I cited the textbook from the bus driver course fluently, wiping danish crumbs off of the table and onto my plate.

Flask slapped me on the back.

"He has a ticket alright, Ishmael. A weekly pass. He can ride around as much as he pleases for a week."

I glanced around the table to see if anyone was about to burst out laughing, but everyone looked serious.

"Well, where does the man go? Where does he get off?"

"Nowhere," Flask stated flatly. "He doesn't get off the bus, Ishmael. He just disappears before the last run of the night."

I thought again that my language skills weren't good enough, and that I wasn't understanding what they were trying to tell me.

"Disappears? Do you mean that you don't have the time to follow where he gets off?"

"We've kept an eye on him alright," butted in Stubb again, who had been driving line 15 for the past two years. "He doesn't get off the bus. He disappears."

Don't believe everything you're being told, I repeated silently inside my head. They were up to something.

The door opened and more drivers came in. They lined up in front of the counter for coffee and snacks, their keys rattling in their pockets. Flask picked his teeth soberly with a toothpick, then shifted into a more comfortable position on the worn-out fake leather couch.

"Disappears, you say?" I said, just to say something.

"Tomorrow you'll see," Flask said, suddenly seeming to have become tired of the conversation.

"We didn't believe it either, until we saw it with our own eyes," Stubb said, glanced at his watch, and made to leave.

The next morning I drove the empty line 15 bus, still chilly inside after the night, to the southern terminal stop, which was located on the edge of a suburban neighborhood. The stop was marked by a dusty shelter that had been tilted over by ground frost. Bolted onto the wall of the shelter was a trash can overflowing with garbage. Houses with hedgerows, lawns, and trees spread out in every direction from the stop. I turned the long bus, swaying, from one dirt road onto the next, and here and there the lowest branches of linden scratched at its roof and windows. A dark, thick spruce hedge cast shade on the bus stop. A robin sang in the branches of one spruce. I opened the window and listened. The bird's melancholy song brought to my mind the misty winter mornings of my native land, and sad memories clamored into my mind. I pushed them aside and tried to concentrate on the shift ahead of me. I made sure that the windshield wipers were working, as the weather forecasts had promised showers.

I didn't want to admit to myself that I was nervous, that in my mind I was quietly expecting a strange man in a black coat to emerge from between the houses and forge his way to the bus stop. I didn't see anyone, though. The houses looked deserted, many of them had the curtains drawn. I assumed that the inhabitants were still sleeping behind them.

I adjusted the seat into a better position. I could remember how every sound had echoed in the half-empty bus depot a quarter of an hour before: doors opening, coughs, footsteps. I had run into Stubb in the depot, who true-to-form didn't say much, just sucked with hollow cheeks on his morning cigarette, ground it into the asphalt with his shoe, and then climbed on the number 7. He had, however, called out, "Say hello to Ahab," from his window and winked at me.

Last night, before falling asleep, I thought about the story I had heard in the break room and was now almost certain that Ahab didn't exist, that the whole story had been a tall tale. Yet, as I was eating breakfast, I thought that Flask was no joker and wouldn't have taken part in any pranks or practical jokes.

I looked at my watch. Five to six. I made sure the fare machine was working properly. Then I opened and closed the bus doors one more time and also made sure that the radio was working. I pulled the bus out of the stop and heard the dirt road crackling under the tires.

By the time I reached the market square downtown, the bus was already half-filled with passengers. There were school children and people going to work, as well as a few people going early to the market. I had watched silently as the bus filled up. A couple of older men had climbed aboard, but honestly through the front door, and none of them looked like the passenger my colleagues had described.

Many of the passengers got off at the market square, and bus was left almost empty. Right after I left the bus stop, I had to halt at a red light. I leaned my elbows on the steering wheel and absent-mindedly watched the people crossing the road. When the light turned green a moment later, I put the bus in gear and accelerated through the intersection in order to turn right at the next crossroad and continue away from the center of the city. When I eyed the mirror a moment later, a small, narrow-faced man was sitting on the backseat staring out of the side window. He had black, close-cropped hair, and he had buried his hands in the pockets of his thick overcoat. I felt my palms, which were gripping the steering wheel, start to sweat: the man had to be Ahab.

The man was still sitting in the bus when I stopped at the terminal stop at the northern fringe of the city. Without taking my eyes off the mirror for a second, I pushed the button to open the middle and back doors. It was just as I had expected: the two other passengers that had come to the terminal stop got off the bus, but the man on the backseat stayed where he was without making any signs of leaving. I closed the doors, opened the gate to the cab, and made my way down the aisle to the back of the bus. As I got closer, the man seemed to stir from deep thoughts and looked at me. His black eyes burned like two glowing embers.

"Last stop," I said and halted a few yards away from the man, pretending to look out the window.

"I know," he replied simply and gave me a warm smile. I thought I recognized a hint of a foreign accent in his speech, but that didn't make us any closer in this world. I looked him over in silence for a while, then put my hands in my pockets and gave him a polite smile.

"Excuse me, but where are you going?"

"Nowhere. I'm just riding back and forth."

He's not much of a talker, I thought, but nevertheless decided to ask him some more questions.

"I see, just riding around. I'm sorry, but did you show me your ticket when you climbed aboard?"

The smile on his face widened. Dozens of creases and wrinkles formed on his face, and he rummaged around his coat pocket with his right hand for a while.

"I do have a ticket. Here."

I knew without looking that it was a weekly pass. The date of purchase showed that it was valid. I passed the ticket back to the man, and he put it back in his pocket with leisurely gestures. Then he nodded his head and said, "Shouldn't you let those people in?"

I glanced back. Passengers had gathered behind the front door, peering at us. I noticed that it had started to rain. Raindrops had speckled the pavement of the turnaround, and the rain was staring to come down harder. The people standing outside were flipping up their coat collars, and one of them knocked sharply on the door.

I turned on my heels and hurried to let them in.

"So, do you believe me now?" Flask asked me in the break room that afternoon. We were again sitting at our regular table, this time just the two of us. I'd told him about the passenger. He didn't seem to be surprised by what he heard, just spooned the remains of a dissolved sugar lump from bottom of his coffee cup into his mouth.

"So he was still in the bus when you changed shifts with Starbuck?"

"Yes. He sat there for over seven hours. From six-thirty to two. You would think that…hmm, how do you say it…? The thing that goes numb?"

Flask raised his eyes from his coffee cup and creased his forehead a moment with a helpful expression on his face.

"Ass?"

"No, a polite word…"

"Posterior?"

"Yes, that's it: you'd think that his posterior would go numb."

Flask took the spoon from his cup and placed it next to the cup on the table.

"So he rode the line eight times end to end?"

"Yes."

"With a weekly pass?"

"With a weekly pass."

Flask pushed his driver's cap back on his head and scratched his forehead. Then he pulled the cap back into place and said:

"Well, if the man has nothing better to do than sit in a transport service bus day in, day out, then let him sit. There's no harm in that."

I thought how wonderful it was that I now knew what "day in, day out" meant, but I kept quiet.

"Believe me, Ishmael, he's going to stay glued to that seat right through Starbuck's shift. And then he'll disappear sometime during the last round."

"And reappear again in the morning?"

"Probably."

I took a bite out of my cheese sandwich and washed it down with some coffee. The door opened, Flask nodded to the drivers walking in with the shoulders of their jackets covered in raindrops. A few yards away, on the other side of the window, rain was gushing relentlessly down the drainpipe. A gusty wind tore at the two-foot tall birch sapling wedged in a crack in the pavement.

The next morning, I got the bus out of the depot early and drove an extra round through the empty city, while quarrelsome black-headed gulls were flocking on the dew-spotted streets and the last partygoers of the night were weaving their way home.

This time, I noticed Ahab after I had driven only a few hundred yards, and I hadn't even stopped yet. He had chosen the same seat as yesterday and was yawning widely without bothering to cover his mouth. Dark stubble was sprouting along his narrow jawline, and he had flipped up the collar of his coat to shield his cheeks. It looked as if he had just woken up, skipped his breakfast, and grabbed his coat from the rack while running to the door. I thought I could almost see a hint of striped pajamas underneath his coat.

I noticed through the mirror that there was a large, white, rectangular object in the aisle next to him. As we were still in the suburban neighborhood and there were no other passengers in the bus, I thought it best to pull over onto the side of the road. As I drew closer, I saw that the white, slightly over three feet high and two feet wide object was a refrigerator.

"Good morning," I said brusquely and tried to remember whether there had been anything about traveling with a refrigerator in the driver course.

"Morning, morning," he replied and flashed a quick smile. I nodded my head toward the refrigerator with a frown.

"What's that?"

"A refrigerator," he answered. "Battery powered."

"And you're transporting it on the bus?"

A perplexed look crossed his wrinkled face.

"How else would I transport it? I don't own a car."

"Home-delivery wasn't included in the price?"

"Included in the price…? Ah, you think that I've bought the fridge. I haven't bought it. That is, not now, but earlier, of course."

A thought crept to my mind that my colleagues had paid the old man to participate in their prank after all. Maybe I'd be caught on candid camera. I glanced around suspiciously, and decided to leave the old man alone.

"Don't block the whole aisle with your fridge," I mumbled and turned around to go back. I heard a polite voice behind me:

"It's not in anyone's way. You can pass by it quite comfortably, as you can see. And if the bus gets crowded, I can always pick it up and put it on my lap. It hardly weighs anything. No need to worry. I promise that it won't be a nuisance to anyone."

I stopped. Irritation was still trying to surface. I counted to ten in my head, before I turned around.

"Where did you come aboard?"

"I do have a ticket."

The man showed me the same ticket that I'd already seen the day before. I checked the date of expiry: still four more days left.

"Are you going to ride the bus all day again?"

He reacted to my stern tone of voice by straightening his posture and rubbing his left earlobe.

"Maybe. Who knows."

I gave him a piercing look.

"All day with the refrigerator?"

"I have my provisions in there. So that I can keep my strength up. Yesterday I got hungry half way through the trip."

We sized each other up with our gazes. Then he said:

"I'm sorry, but could we get moving again. We don't want to be very late. Otherwise there'll be trouble."

I glanced at my watch and swallowed my anger. I made my way back behind the wheel without a word, started the engine, and steered the bus down the narrow dirt road, which was lined by a hawthorn hedge. In the mirror, I could see that, in the tightest bends, Ahab held the refrigerator up with both hands.

I drove line 15 for the next couple of weeks. Ahab appeared in the bus every day, and soon I had grown so accustomed to him that I didn't even remember that he was sitting there in the back-most seat. In addition to the refrigerator, he had hauled a battery-powered portable television with a VCR into the bus. There he then sat, watching programs he had taped. Although he didn't look at all like a sports fan, he seemed to take pleasure in quick interviews with athletes. He was especially captivated by the interviews conducted right after an athlete's performance, when they would be lying, spread-eagled, on the ground, hair glued to their temples in sweaty bundles, spit dripping from their mouths, panting and spattering words into the microphone, having given their all. Now and then he would open his refrigerator, which seemed to carry a never-ending supply of food in it: sometimes he would shovel yoghurt into his mouth, sometimes cold carrot pancakes or kidney pies, at other times he'd have a frankfurter or half a bratwurst in his mitt, and the sputter of his plastic mustard bottle could be heard all the way in the front of the bus.

I soon noted that the other passengers didn't react to Ahab in any way. We concluded that either they didn't see or hear him, or they just didn't know he existed at all. It looked as if he existed only for us, the drivers of line 15.

Later, I transferred to other lines for a while and didn't see Ahab anymore. My colleagues talked about him a great deal, and I always knew the latest turns of events. I heard that he had turned the back of the bus into a cozy cubby hole, had hung curtains on the windows and laid a small, vividly colored rag rug on the floor. He was also drying laundry on a clothesline that he has hung across the aisle between the overhead luggage racks. Stubb said that he had complained to Ahab that he wasn't allowed to take up the space of three people with his belongings. The next day the man had handed over three weekly passes for Stubb to inspect and then had withdrawn to his den with a satisfied grin on his face.

About six months after Ahab had appeared, I sat in the empty bus at the end of line 15. I had never before seen an early fall day as dark as this one: the moping clouds were indigo, and they had anchored their paunches to the tree tops and squashed the light into a narrow dusk between themselves and the earth. The pouring rain added to the darkness: water roared outside, coursed in the ditches that ran alongside the road, dug furrows into the dirt road, cascaded down from the roof of the bus stop, pattered onto the windows of the bus. On top of everything, it was inauspiciously calm. Even though I had flipped on the high beams, I could barely see more than a yard ahead of me as I sat, hunched over, peering through the windshield, pulling the bus away from the stop. The windshield wipers were flicking as fast as they could, but the water was pouring down so densely that I might as well have turned them off entirely.

In my mind's eye, I could see the roads flooded with water and raft loads of people drifting with the flow, drenched by the gusts of rain and numbed by the cold water, trying to paddle their way toward the middle of the waterway. I saw them trying to prevent their belongings from falling off the raft, from being lost in the whirlpool surrounding them; I saw them trying to tie their things to the logs of their rafts with ropes. Then, in the middle of a cascade of spray, I saw, like a sudden apparition, a large, unmanned raft passing by my eyes. A white refrigerator had been tied down onto it with a dozen wrist-thick ropes.

At that moment I was overcome by an inexplicable, oppressive certainty that Ahab would no longer appear in the bus.

When I finally made it to the stop by the market square, he wasn't in his usual place. I didn't hear the familiar sounds from the back of the bus: the panting of sweaty athletes, the bland excuses, the interviewer's comments, the congratulating or the consoling phrases. There was no striped rug, blue curtains, or shirts and socks hung out to dry on the clothesline. Moreover, there was no Ahab. In a word: the bus felt unfamiliar and bleak.

My mind was sad and heavy. Outside the rain seemed to be coming down harder than before. Every now and then, the raindrops that struck the ground in a glimmering shroud froze into hailstones the size of fingertips, which drummed on the roof and sides of the bus only to transform back into water in the next moment. The bus plowed down the river of the road, the wheels raised tall waves off the streets, which folded back down over the sidewalks.

On my way back, visibility was zero, and I drove at a snail's pace. From time to time I could distinguish a flash of light from the headlights of oncoming cars. The road to the suburban neighborhood cut through a small field, which the rain had turned into a seething expanse of mud. As I reached the center of the field, something suddenly caught my attention up ahead on the left, behind the curtain of water. I hit the brakes and stopped the bus, as there was no one aboard. I left the headlights on and carefully cracked the front window on the driver's side. In the field, about fifty yards from the road, there was a white patch. I stared at it for several minutes, but there was no doubt about it: at an angle in the middle of the expanse of mud stood Ahab's refrigerator!

I snatched my raincoat off the back of the seat, pushed the front door of the bus open, and stepped outside. It was as if I had run into a wall: the rain made it hard to breath and the raindrops felt like needle points. I struggled to get my coat on, but the wind ripped it from my hands. I was already soaking wet before I lost my balance and slid on my side down into the ditch, into a flood of murky, cold silt that enveloped me; it pulled me in deeper, it bit my ears and scraped my nose and nipped at my gums, it surrounded me like the cold ring of a well.

I pushed myself sputtering up out of the ditch, with soggy hay in my hair, my eyes and mouth full of clay, and crawled to the field that had become a mud gruel, a gurgling porridge of clay sludge. I sank into it up to my ankles, and it pulled at me, pulled the shoes off my feet and coiled its cold shackles around my ankles, which ached and throbbed, and I fell, slipped, and slid, until I finally felt solid ground beneath my feet. I pulled my clay-caked hair out of my eyes and saw that the refrigerator stood in the flooded field like a gigantic lump of sugar.

Only a few more yards, I thought, and with shaking legs and aching ankles waded my way to the fridge. It was upright, but slightly tilted, one of its corners had sunk into the mud, splitting the current in two. The rain cascaded off the white surface of the refrigerator and seethed on the ground around its base. I swallowed water, clay rasped between my teeth. I tugged the hair from my eyes, the force of the rain made me gasp for breath. I wrapped my arms around the refrigerator and flexed my muscles—its weight didn't even budge. I straightened my back for a while, tried to steady my breath. Then I bent over and embraced the refrigerator a second time. I lifted with my legs, even though they would get stuck in the mud at any moment. Eventually, after exerting myself to the limit of my strength, I felt the refrigerator move, the clay holding it wheezed. I flexed one more time, and the earth released its prize with a slurp.

The journey back to the bus lasted an eternity. It was my destination, the bus on the desolate road, eerie and empty, the cabin lit, the headlights on, the windshield wipers flicking, the front door open. Step by step it came closer, grew in size, called to me.

When I at last reached the bus, I noticed that rain had splashed in through the door and drenched the red carpet in the entryway. I climbed the first step and rested one of the corners of the fridge on it. I panted there for a while, my heart pounding in my chest. Gritting my teeth, I tightened my grasp, wrenched myself inside, and with my last strength, my consciousness nearly fading, I carried the refrigerator to the back of the bus, to the spot where Ahab usually kept it.

Then I sat and rested for many minutes. My eyes closed, clutching the armrests of the seat. Dead tired, cold, with an empty mind.

At last I had to get up, to hold out a little while longer.

I bent over the refrigerator.

The door opened with ease. The rubber seals had held, no water had leaked in. The light turned on after flickering for a moment. I dropped to my knees in front of the refrigerator.

It was empty.

Empty, apart from a large container made from pallid green glass with a tin lid fixed to the top with screws.

The container was filled with a golden liquid.

In the liquid, head down, floated Ahab.

His shrunken, naked body, its pale limbs bent into a fetal position. I stared straight into his wrinkled face. His mouth and eyes hung open, and there was an astonished, melancholy look in his eyes. From his slender neck hung a thin metal chain, at the end of which, just inches from the bottom of the container, dangled a small, metal Star of David. In his left hand he still clasped a drenched weekly bus pass issued by the city transport service.

Author's Note

I know that in my writing there is a dark undercurrent which some readers might find hard to take, even repulsive. It is part of my world as an artist and has its roots, I suppose, in the unconscious levels of my psyche. In my art, I always try to filter that black, uncanny undercurrent into my work, because I think it runs in every person. As a result, not everything that I write is pleasant or comforting to read; sometimes my style is blatant and bold, even blunt, and perhaps disturbing. That is exactly what I love in it, one of the main reasons why I write. (And also one of the reasons why I am not, and will never become, a mainstream writer, entertaining enough to capture "the soul of the masses").

ABOUT THE AUTHOR:

Jyrki Vainonen is an award-winning Finnish author who is renowned for his Finnish translations of the works of Seamus Heaney, Jonathan Swift and William Shakespeare. He has lived in Ireland and wrote his licentiate thesis on Swift's Irish pamphlets. Vainonen's first collection of short stories was awarded the Helsingin Sanomat Literature Prize and his work has been featured in such iconic collections as the *Dedalus Book of Finnish Fantasy*.

ABOUT THE TRANSLATORS:

Anna Volmari is a Finnish, internationally educated freelance translator. **J. Robert Tupasela** is a Finnish-Australian, New-York-raised translator. Between them they have two decades of translation experience and have lived in five countries on three continents. They collaborate on literary translations between Finnish and English, including English translations of Finnish authors Leena Krohn, Jyrki Vainonen and Carita Forsgren and Finnish translations of two crime novels by James Thompson. They live in Helsinki with two cats and a mountain of books.

Hildi Hawkins is a writer and translator and the London Editor of Books from Finland. She is also the editor of *things magazine*, a journal of writings about objects, their pasts, presents and futures.

OTHER BOOKS AVAILABLE
FROM CHEEKY FRAWG

Cheeky Frawg has made a strong commitment to Nordic/Scandinavian fiction, reflected in our current offerings…

Print and E-book

Jagannath by Karin Tidbeck. Enter the strange and wonderful world of Swedish sensation Karin Tidbeck with this feast of darkly fantastical short stories. Whether through the falsified historical record of the uniquely weird Swedish creature known as the "Pyret" or the title story, "Jagannath," about a biological ark in the far future, Tidbeck's unique imagination will enthrall, amuse, and unsettle you. How else to describe a collection that includes "Cloudberry Jam," a story that opens with the line "I made you in a tin can"? Winner of the Crawford Award and shortlisted for the World Fantasy Award. Introduction by Elizabeth Hand.

Datura by Leena Krohn, translated by Anna Volmari and Juha Tupasela. Our narrator works as an editor and writer for a magazine specializing in bringing oddities to light, a job that sends her exploring through a city that becomes by degrees ever less familiar. From a sunrise of automated cars working in silent precision to a possible vampire, she discovers that reality may not be as logical as you think—and that people are both odder and more ordinary as they might seem. Especially if you're eating datura seeds. Especially when the legendary Voynich Manuscript is involved. Where will it all end? Pushed by the mysterious owner of the magazine, our narrator may wind up somewhere very strange indeed. "*Datura* is luminous–at once a secret history of losers, dreamers, and quacks, and a lyrical argument on the nature of reality. I thoroughly enjoyed it." – Sofia Samatar, *A Stranger in Olondria*

E-book only

It Came from the North edited by Desirina Boskovich. This anthology of Finnish fantasy features fiction from Jyrki Vainonen, Leena Krohn, Johanna Sinisalo, Hannu Rajaniemi, Anne Leinonen, Tiina Raevaara and many more—including Pasi Ilmari Jaaskelainen, author of the critically acclaimed *The Rabbit Back Literature Society*. What will you find within these pages? A photographer stumbles on a wounded troll, and attempts to nurse it back to health. A lonely girl discovers the flames in the family smithy are tied to an ancient portal between worlds. A peculiar swamp holds restorative powers, for its avian and human inhabitants alike. *It Came From the North* offers a diverse selection of fifteen fantastical tales including stories from some of Finland's most respected writers, alongside up-and-coming talents who are redefining the rules of contemporary literature.

Tainaron by Leena Krohn. The classic novel by an iconic Finnish author, a finalist for the World Fantasy Award. Tainaron: a city like no other, populated by talking insects, as observed by the nameless narrator, who is far from home. A World Fantasy Award finalist. Afterword by Matthew Cheney. "The novel contains scenes of startling beauty and strangeness that change how the reader sees the world. Krohn effortlessly melds the literal with the metaphorical, so that the narrator's exploration of the city through its inhabitants encompasses both the speculation of science fiction and the resonant symbolism of the surreal." – Locus.

Forthcoming in 2014

The Leena Krohn Omnibus. An unmissable and unstoppable thousand-page celebration of iconic Finnish author Leena Krohn. This epic volume, to be issued in hardcover, trade paperback, and e-book editions, will include the short novels *Pereat Mundus, Tainaron, Dona Quixote & Other Citizens,* and *Gold of Ophir,* among others, in addition to a selection of short fiction, essays, and poetry. The omnibus will also feature appreciations by other writers.

CPSIA information can be obtained at www.ICGtesting.com
Printed in the USA
LVOW13s1015081013

355949LV00002B/334/P